LADY COLT

When word comes through that two of the infamous Wallace brothers have been spotted in Indian Territory, Liberty Mercer — only the second woman ever to become a Deputy US Marshal — rides out to arrest them. But things don't go to plan, and Liberty finds herself left in the desert to die. Fortunately, rescue comes in the unlikely shape of a young girl named Clementina, on the run herself — from a stepmother who happens to be the matriarch of the Wallace gang . . .

STEVE HAYES

LADY COLT

Complete and Unabridged

LINFORD
Leicester

First published in Great Britain in 2012 by
Sixgold Book
London

First Linford Edition
published 2014
by arrangement with
Sixgold Book
London

A catalogue record for this book is available
from the British Library.

ISBN 978–1–4448–1851–2

Published by
F. A. Thorpe (Publishing)
Anstey, Leicestershire

Set by Words & Graphics Ltd.
Anstey, Leicestershire
Printed and bound in Great Britain by
T. J. International Ltd., Padstow, Cornwall

This book is printed on acid-free paper

To Ema Sadek
This one's for you

1

It was a hot, windless evening and the election celebration was in full swing.

The rider galloping along Front Street could hear the fiddle, banjo and Ozark harp music, mingled with raucous laughter, coming from the town hall ahead. There were horses and buckboards tied up out front. The rider reined up beside them and quickly dismounted. Hitching his sweaty horse to the rail, he slapped the trail dust from his clothes and hurried inside.

The main reception room of the large wood-frame building was lit by numerous hanging lanterns. Their muted yellow light illuminated the red, white and blue confetti sprinkled on the floor and all the decorative streamers and banners strung between the rafters that congratulated Mayor Robert 'Bob' Justin on being reelected. The noisy, happy crowd dancing the Texas two-step below the banners was made up of townspeople, farmers and cattlemen whose spreads surrounded Clearwater, a small but fast-growing town in recently-incorporated Oklahoma Territory.

The rider, a short wiry cowboy named Calvin Eads, elbowed his way through the throng of onlookers watching the dancers, and looked around for the marshal. Smiling couples went sashaying past him, blocking his view. Frustrated, he pushed people aside and hurried to the makeshift podium.

Climbing onto it, he told the musicians to stop playing and faced the angry dancers. 'Quiet, everybody! Hold it down! Quiet!'

'What the hell you doing, Cal?' Mayor Justin shouted at him.

'Get down from there!' yelled another man.

'I will, I will,' Eads promised, 'soon as I find the marshal.'

'He's not here,' Liberty Mercer said.

She squeezed through the crowd, up to the podium, adding: 'Marshal Thompson's on a train back to Guthrie.'

'Damn.' Eads searched the faces staring up at him. 'Where's Sheriff Hagen?'

'In bed with a fever. Why? *Why?*' Liberty repeated when Eads didn't answer. 'What do you need him for?'

Eads hesitated and shuffled uncomfortably.

Liberty climbed onto the podium and looked him challengingly in the eye. She was a tall, lithe, wholesomely attractive woman in her early twenties with wide-set golden brown eyes that, depending on the situation, could sparkle with humor or turn wintry hard. Her tanned farm-fresh face was splashed with freckles that belied her often taciturn nature, her strong resolute jaw suggested stubbornness, and years in the sun had bleached her brown hair yellow as lamp light. Usually clad in old faded denims, cotton shirt and boots, with a cedar-handled Colt

.45 holstered on her hip, tonight in honor of the Mayor's re-election she wore an ankle-length, powder-blue gingham dress and new, too-tight button-up shoes that had given her blisters.

'I asked you a question, Cal. Why do you need to talk to the marshal or the sheriff?'

''Cause I seen two of the Wallace brothers, Josh and Caleb.'

That got everyone's attention, even the folks gathered at the punch table.

'Where?' Liberty demanded.

'Okfuskee Flats.'

'Sure it was them?'

''Course I'm sure. They was playing poker in the Lucky Deuce. That's why I high-tailed it over here.'

The room went quiet. Liberty felt everyone's eyes on her. As a recently appointed Deputy U.S. Marshal and only the second woman to ever hold such an authoritative position, she knew what her obligations were and she was more than willing to fulfill them — it was just that she loved dancing and lately, since becoming a Federal law officer, hadn't had time for it.

'Go home,' she told Eads. 'I'll handle it.'

'But — '

'I *said* . . . I'll handle it.'

It was an order, not a suggestion, and Eads knew better than to argue. 'Sure thing, deputy,' he said lamely and turned away.

But Mayor Justin, who like most men was against women being lawmen, stabbed a finger at Liberty. 'Okfuskee Flats,' he reminded grimly, 'is in Indian Territory.'

'I'm aware of that, Bob,' she said quietly. 'But it's in my jurisdiction and all five of the Wallace brothers are wanted for murder, rape and robbery.'

'I know that, dammit, but — '

'If I was you, Liberty,' Walt Neuhauser broke in, 'I'd be waiting till morning. Maybe by then Will Hagen will be well enough to ride with you.'

Liberty smiled — a thin, tight-lipped

smile that never reached her gold-flecked brown eyes. 'You questioning my sand, Walt?'

'You know better than that,' he growled.

'My ability, then?'

'If I hadn't thought you were capable, woman, I wouldn't have put in a good word for you with Marshal Thompson.'

'Then what's chewing on you?'

The blacksmith shrugged his massive sloping shoulders. 'I just figure two's got a better chance of throwing a rope on the Wallace boys than — '

'Maybe we should round up a posse,' Mayor Justin said. He was a short, big-bellied man with curly white hair and a baritone voice that had won him the votes of Clearwater's widows. 'There's a five hundred dollar reward for any member of the Wallace gang — dead or alive.'

'Who's gonna head up that posse,' a man asked Liberty. ' — you?'

'Who else?'

As one, the men standing among the onlookers immediately turned away.

Stung by their rejection, Liberty said: 'I don't need a posse, Mayor. I can bring those two misfits in by myself.' She turned to Eads, adding: 'Anyone see you riding away from Okfuskee Flats?'

'Uh-uh. Streets were empty.'

'What about when you were in the Lucky Deuce?'

Eads shook his head. 'I was by myself at the bar, near the door. Soon as I spotted the Wallace boys I got the hell out of there. Tell you this, though: if you're figuring on arresting them, you best get moving now, 'cause I heard Josh tell the barkeep that they was planning on joining up with their brothers come sunup.'

Without hesitation Liberty said to the Mayor: 'Tell Sheriff Hagen where I've gone and then wire Marshal Thompson the same news. Tell them both I'll be back by tomorrow nightfall with the prisoners.' She was gone before anyone could argue.

2

Liberty lived alone in a small rented green-and-white clapboard house a mile east of town. Tempted to go home and change into riding clothes, she realized time was of the essence and instead hurried to the sheriff's office.

Here, she armed herself with a Winchester Model '92 and a Colt Frontier .44–40 revolver, both of which used the same caliber cartridges and were part of the office arsenal. Next she grabbed a box of ammunition and two pairs of wrist-irons from the desk drawer. In the same drawer was a half-empty bottle of Old Crow. She was not against enjoying an occasional whiskey, though she wasn't a hardened drinker by any means, and she'd stared down danger many times. But she knew that arresting Caleb and Josh Wallace was the most life-threatening assignment she'd ever tackled alone and wondered if a little extra fortification might not help calm her nerves.

She started to pull the cork then instinctively decided she didn't need false courage and returned the bottle to the drawer. Then stuffing everything into her saddlebag, she hurried out and crossed the street to Logan's Livery.

Outside the stable a massive, coarse-furred white dog stood drinking at the public water trough. Badly in need of a bath, it resembled an all-white Saint Bernard with long powerful legs and a thick feathery tail that when it became aroused curled over its back. Ownerless and nicknamed Trouble, it roamed the town, befriending no one, content to wander at its own pace, feeding itself either by hunting or from whatever scraps were thrown its way by various restaurant and saloon owners. No one knew where the dog slept at night and only a few remembered that it had appeared out of the mountains to the north three years ago. Its breed had been a mystery until one winter a French miner passing through Clearwater claimed he'd seen similar-looking dogs in the snowy Pyrenees Mountains in Southern France and Northern Spain, where the Basque shepherds used them to guard their flocks against wolves and eagles. From then on the townspeople had taken pride in the big Pyrenees Mountain dog and Trouble had become a welcome fixture.

It looked up as Liberty walked past, its fierce dark-brown eyes watching her suspiciously until it was satisfied that she meant it no harm, and then went on drinking.

Liberty entered the stables and looked around for the hostler, Luke Logan. The old man wasn't there. Guessing he was enjoying the celebration going on at the town hall, she saddled her leggy ill-tempered buckskin, Regret, and rode off.

Once out of town, she kicked the horse into a mile-consuming lope and headed west, out across the wasteland toward Okfuskee Flats. She knew the ride to Indian Territory would take much of the night and was glad she'd eaten dinner before going to the dance. Drifting clouds hid the moon and most of the stars, the darkness hampering her visibility. Fortunately she'd ridden over this terrain before, and knowing the ground was uneven and full of black-tail prairie dog holes she prepared herself for any sudden stumble or skittishness by her horse.

Regret, so-named because everyone had told her that she'd regret buying him, possessed fine stamina and could run down most horses — attributes that any lawman would appreciate. But the buckskin was also unpredictable and inclined to be irascible. Without warning, and for no apparent reason, it could turn mean or paranoid. Then it became scared of everything from wind-blown tumbleweeds to shadows or birds flying in front of it, causing it to shy and sometimes buck. These traits, along with its tendency to bite even a friendly hand had so angered previous owners, each one soon resold the horse for less than they'd paid for it.

But Liberty had taken to the buckskin right away and happily paid the seventy-five-dollar asking price. She knew the horse was worth at least twice that and was willing to put up with its quirky behavior. She also sensed they were two of a kind: hell, despite her well-mannered upbringing and education at St. Marks, a convent in Las Cruces, New Mexico she could be irascible and unpredictable herself.

As a child brought up by the Mercer family, all of whom had been killed by raiding Comancheros, she had been inherently shy. But as she'd grown older, she'd learned to hide her shyness behind a façade of feisty, stubborn defiance — a recipe that had not only earned her a reputation for being bluntly honest and fearless, but had scared off all the local bachelors who'd arrived three years ago during the '89 Land Run.

This was fine with Liberty. She wasn't looking to get hitched but instead was determined to make a name for herself as a Federal lawman.

Capturing two of the infamous Wallace brothers' gang would be a first step toward building her résumé. She knew it wouldn't be easy. All five of the brothers were ruthless, lowlife scum who robbed banks, stagecoaches and trains and killed without compunction. But danger came with the job and Liberty, undaunted, knew if she was going to have any chance at all of arresting them, without getting shot, she had to find a way to get the drop on them.

How?

That was the question.

3

Okfuskee Flats was an outlaw haven. With a population of less than fifty, it stood in the middle of the badlands — a squalid collection of tents, dugouts and sod houses, a saloon, livery stable and a general store that openly sold stolen goods. Like the rest of Indian Territory there was no official law here and shootings were common, which is why a crude-painted sign over the entrance to Boot Hill proudly claimed to have more inhabitants than the town itself.

Liberty rode past the dismal scattering of cheap headstones and wooden crosses and entered town. The rutted dirt street that ran between the gambling tents and false-fronted stores was empty. Slowing the buckskin to a walk, she rode cautiously up to the Lucky Deuce, an old, wood-framed, two-story building with rooms upstairs in which over-the-hill whores pleasured men for loose change.

Before dismounting, Liberty looked carefully about her. All the tents and buildings were closed and the only light came from the saloon. Though dawn was gradually yellowing the cloudy gray sky there were still a few customers in the Lucky Deuce: Liberty could hear their coarse drunken laughter and the faint jingling of their spurs as they walked on the plank flooring.

Taking a deep breath to calm her nerves, she dismounted, wrapped the reins around the hitch-rail and took the Colt .44 and two pairs of wrist-irons from her saddlebag. Tucking the gun and the wrist-irons into her belt, she pulled the Winchester from its scabbard and levered a shell into the chamber.

The other horses tied to the rail nickered and stirred restlessly. Not wanting to attract attention, Liberty walked carefully around them, stepped onto the crude plank-walk and peered over the top of the batwing doors.

The barkeep was stretched out asleep on top of the bar, his loud snoring hiding the low conversation going on at one of the rear tables. A few sleepy onlookers, including two fat, heavily-rouged, sorry-looking whores, stood gathered about four hard-looking men drinking whiskey and playing poker by the light of a flickering candle.

Liberty recognized two of the players from the wanted posters pinned on the wall of the marshal's office: Josh and Caleb Wallace. The other two men she didn't recognize, but by their unkempt beards, trail-soiled clothes, sweat-stained hats and well-used six-guns poking from their tied-down holsters she guessed they were either gunmen, bounty hunters or members of the Wallace gang.

Despite the cool dawn breeze blowing in off the wasteland, Liberty felt herself sweating. Rifle cocked, she entered the saloon and slowly walked alongside the bar toward the poker players.

At the end of the bar she stopped,

16

leveled her rifle at the Wallace brothers and said grimly: 'Game's over, gentlemen.'

Everyone around the table froze for an instant then slowly turned and looked at Liberty.

Whomever they expected to see, it sure as hell wasn't her. Despite the well-oiled Winchester in her hands and the long-barreled Colt tucked in her belt, the sight of a pretty young woman in a pale blue gingham dress and button-up shoes, with pinned-back sun-colored hair and lips lightly reddened by rouge was more amusing than threatening.

Caleb, the younger of the two Wallace brothers, grinned, showing broken snuff-stained teeth. 'Well, now, look at what we got here, boys — a real live lady. You fall off a caboose, school teacher?'

Everyone howled.

'Must be lost,' Josh Wallace joked.

'Must be,' agreed Caleb, 'since we don't got no school.'

'I am not lost,' Liberty said.

'Then who are you and what in sweet Jesus you doin' here?'

'Name's Mercer. Deputy U.S. Marshal Liberty Mercer. And you and your brother are under arrest.'

Everyone laughed drunkenly.

'Hear that, boys?' Caleb grinned. 'Lady Marshal here says me'n Josh is under arrest.'

More drunken laughter.

'You sure is pretty for a marshal, honey,' one of the whores said.

'Yeah,' said the other. 'You talk pretty too. And I just loove your Sunday-come-morning dress.'

The snide compliment, accompanied by giggles, made Liberty burn. But bickering with whores was beneath her and she kept her concentration fixed on the outlaws.

'If you're a deputy marshal, teacher,' Josh Wallace said. 'Where's your badge?'

Liberty looked down at her dress and realized she'd not worn her shield to the Mayor's dance, hence wasn't wearing it now.

'I don't need a badge to clap irons on you two losers,' she said. 'Now, on your feet and unbuckle your gun-belts.'

There was a tense silence as everyone swapped uneasy glances. Then Caleb took a dip of snuff, wedged it between his gum and cheek and grinned at Liberty.

'Aw, c'mon, girlie,' he said mockingly. 'you ain't fooling nobody.'

'You one of them back-east stage actresses, honey?' one whore asked.

'I hear they got a real theater over to Guthrie,' said the other whore. 'With 'lectric lights and a' orchestra and everything.'

'I'm no actress,' Liberty said tersely.

'Then how come you talk so fancy?'

'Ever heard of schooling?'

That stumped them.

'If you ain't no actress, then who put you up to this?' Caleb demanded.

'No one. I'm here as an officer of the law.'

'Ain't no such thing as a lady lawman an' you know it.'

'What I know,' Liberty said, angered by their disrespect, 'is you're behind the times and your ignorance is going to cost you. Now,' she wagged her rifle at the brothers, 'quit flapping your tongues and do as I say. Both of you get up and unbuckle those belts. Or I swear to Moses I'll gun you down.'

Again there was a tense, uneasy silence. Then Caleb spat snuff-juice on the floor and chuckled, as if he'd just figured it out, and pointing to the sleeping bar-keep whispered something that made his brother laugh. Both got up and mock-ingly stuck out their wrists.

'Please don't shoot, marshal,' Caleb begged. 'Me'n my brother, here, we won't give you no trouble. Will we, Josh?'

'No, ma'am,' Josh said. 'Here, teach — I mean marshal. Put them irons on me 'fore I get to shaking so bad I piss my pants.' He laughed and everyone but Liberty laughed with him.

Ignoring their mocking laughter, she pulled the wrist-irons from her belt and threw them on the table. 'Put them on,' she snapped.

'Here, Caleb,' the fatter of the two whores said, 'let me help you, honey.' She fastened the irons on his extended wrists, while the other whore did the same to Josh.

'Now, what?' Caleb asked, amused.

Liberty turned to the whores. 'Throw their guns on the floor. Do it,' she barked as they hesitated. 'Now.'

The whores grudgingly obeyed.

Liberty kept her rifle trained on the Wallace brothers, at the same time never taking her eyes off the two men seated beside them. 'You do the same,' she ordered.

''Mean you're arresting us too?' the taller of the two men said.

'Only if you poke your nose in,' Liberty warned.

'Hell, teacher, why would we do that?' the shorter man said. He jokingly laid his six-gun on the table and winked at his partner to do the same. 'We ain't fools enough to buck no big bad

Deputy U.S. Marshal.'

The taller man, a bearded gunman with narrow pale eyes, laid his Colt .45 down then a second later jokingly pretended to grab for it.

Liberty fired a single shot, the bullet splintering the table an inch from his fingers.

He jerked his hand back, cursing her. 'Damn you, girl!'

Liberty pumped the lever and aimed the rifle at him.

'Try that again, mister, and you'll lose a finger.'

The tall man scowled but didn't move.

Keeping the two men covered Liberty slowly backed up toward the exit, the Wallace brothers in front of her. No one around the table moved. Hoping her luck would hold out until she got her prisoners outside, she kept her finger on the trigger, ready to shoot at the first sign of trouble.

Meanwhile, the shot had awakened the barkeep. He sat up on the bar, groggily rubbing sleep from his blood-shot eyes.

'Hey, what's goin' on?' he asked.

'Keep your face shut,' Liberty told him.

Caleb grinned. 'Don't act like you don't know, Judd.'

'Know what? W-What're you talking about?'

'You got us good,' Josh said. 'Real good. But the joke's over now, Judd. Tell this woman to quit funnin' with us. I want to finish this last hand 'fore me'n Caleb ride out to meet Sloane and the others. Here, honey,' he said, offering his wrists to Liberty, 'can take 'em off now.'

Annoyed that they weren't taking her seriously, Liberty jammed the barrel of her rifle into Josh's belly, doubling him over. 'Get the hell outside,' she ordered. 'Both of you!'

'Judd,' Caleb said angrily, 'this ain't funny no more. Tell this sweet-faced bitch to back off.'

'Boys, I swear I had nothing to do

23

with this,' the barkeep said. 'I ain't never seen this gal before.'

The Wallace brothers glared at Liberty.

'I'm warning you,' Caleb said. 'Take these irons off or I'll — '

Liberty whacked him on the temple with the butt of her rifle. Caleb's eyes rolled up into his head and he collapsed on the floor without a sound.

'Drag him outside,' Liberty told Josh.

'The hell I will!'

She fired and the bullet splintered the planking between his boots.

'Do it,' she warned as he flinched, 'or the next round will take a toe off!' Turning to the others, she added: 'Rest of you stay where you are. I'll put a hole in the first one who shows their face out the door.'

She waited until Josh dragged his brother out of the saloon; then she slowly backed up, her back pushing open the batwing doors, her eyes never leaving the men and women at the poker table.

4

Outside, dawn had arrived. The cloudy sky had turned saffron-yellow with lavender streaks. It was a beautiful sight but Liberty never noticed it. Her gaze was fixed on the Wallace brothers.

Caleb was now conscious and Josh helped him up and led him to their horses.

Stepping up into the saddle, Liberty kept her rifle trained on them while at the same time making sure no one emerged from the saloon.

'Ride,' she told the brothers. 'Go on, dammit. Get going!'

'Gonna be sorry for this,' Caleb growled. 'Soon as I get rid of these irons, I swear I'll make you wish you'd never met me.'

'Save your threats,' Liberty said. 'You're going to need all your energy for the long ride ahead. Now, get!'

Grudgingly, the Wallace boys kicked up their horses and headed out of town. Liberty rode behind them, occasionally looking over her shoulder to see if anyone was following. No one was, and after a mile or so she stopped looking and concentrated on the two outlaws riding ahead of her.

Caleb was the more talkative; but Liberty sensed that Josh was more dangerous. She watched him closely, keeping her right hand resting on the saddle horn only inches from the Colt tucked in her belt.

After a few miles a warm wind sprang up. Liberty saw several dust devils swirling in the distance and now and then tumbleweeds went bouncing past. The buckskin whinnied and eyed them nervously. Liberty spoke soothingly to the skittish horse, trying to calm it down.

It was early morning now. The wind had lessened and came in spurts, kicking up dust around them. The sky had lightened to a muddy color and the sun felt warm on their backs. Liberty, her lips caked with dust, took a swig from her canteen then hooked the strap over her saddle horn.

'What about us?' Caleb said, looking back at her.

'You'll live,' Liberty said. Then as he cursed her: 'Consider it a favor. By the time we get to Clearwater, the heat will have sweated all that cheap whiskey out of you.'

The brothers weren't amused. Caleb fell silent. But Josh hummed softly, tunelessly, as they rode on across the hot flat scrubland. There wasn't a hill or a mountain in sight. It was a harsh desolate land that killed the spirit of most settlers. Only the bravest survived. And even they often wondered if it was worth the effort.

Presently Josh looked back at Liberty, saying: 'You a damn fool, girlie. Even if you do get us to Clearwater, how long you think it'll be 'fore our brothers break us out of that piss-ant little jail?'

'Probably no time at all,' she said.

'But unfortunately for you, they won't get the chance. First thing tomorrow morning Sheriff Hagen and I'll be taking you to Guthrie by train.'

'Guthrie? You hear that big brother?' Caleb said to Josh. 'Teacher says you'n me, we're going on a train ride to the capital.'

Josh grunted but didn't say anything.

They rode on across the silent, barren, monotonously flat wasteland.

Shortly, the wind sprang up again and a dust devil went swirling past. With it came several tumbleweeds, bouncing along like runaway balls. One swept across in front of the buckskin. Regret whinnied shrilly and suddenly reared up, almost unseating Liberty.

She managed to hang on, grabbing its long black mane as the horse came back to earth. 'Blast your eyes,' she cursed. 'Cut it out!'

The buckskin ignored her. Still skittish, it bucked and crab-stepped several times, again almost pitching her from the saddle.

Before she could recover, Josh whirled his horse around and rammed the buckskin, knocking it off its feet. Horse and rider thumped to the ground.

Liberty tried to scramble up but her left leg was trapped under the fallen, panicked buckskin.

Josh, meanwhile, vaulted from the saddle, stumbled, regained his balance and hurled himself at Liberty. Though cuffed, his body pinned her to the dirt. She struggled desperately, but Josh and the weight of the fallen horse kept her pinned.

'Get her gun!' he yelled at his brother, who was already out of the saddle and running toward them.

A moment later, Caleb reached the struggling horse. Stooping, he jerked Liberty's rifle from its scabbard. Then holding the butt between his knees, he levered a shell into the magazine and jammed the barrel against her head.

'Don't move,' he hissed, 'or I'll scatter your brains from here to Kansas.'

Liberty obeyed.

The buckskin at last scrambled to its feet and stood there, eyes fearful, nostrils flared, breathing hard and trembling.

Josh grabbed the Colt .44 from Liberty's belt and stood up. 'Get the keys, little brother.'

Caleb hurried to Liberty's saddle-bags. Digging out the keys from one of them, he quickly unlocked Josh's wrist-irons. Then while Josh kept Liberty covered, Caleb unlocked his own cuffs and tossed them off into the desert.

'Can get up now, teacher,' Josh told Liberty.

Rising, she stood facing them, shaken but fearless.

'Reckon we won't be going on that choo-choo ride with you,' Caleb said, grinning at her.

'Always another train,' she replied grimly.

'Not for us,' Josh said. 'Or you.'

'You can't be that stupid,' Liberty

said. 'Kill a Deputy U.S. Marshal and all hell will come down on you. You and your brother will spend the rest of your lives looking over your shoulder.'

'We're doing that already,' Caleb said. 'Anyways, how the hell we supposed to know you're a marshal? You ain't wearing no badge.'

''Sides,' Josh put in, 'we ain't planning to kill you. We ain't even gonna mess with you. We just gonna ride off and leave you here . . . '

'Yeah, far as we're concerned,' Caleb said, 'we never even seen you.'

'That barkeep and those two whores did,' Liberty reminded. 'You think they won't talk to save their sorry necks?'

'Who's gonna believe two broke-down whores and a fella wanted for beating his wife to death?' Caleb said. 'No sir. When they find you, girlie, everybody's gonna think you fell off your horse an' wandered around till you died of thirst.'

Josh swung up into the saddle and motioned to Caleb. 'C'mon, little brother. Time's a-wasting and we got to hook up with the others.'

Caleb grabbed the reins of Liberty's buckskin, 'So long, teacher,' mounted his own horse and together the two outlaws rode back toward Okfuskee Flats.

5

Liberty watched the Wallace brothers riding away with her horse until they were tiny dots on the wavering horizon and then kicked the dirt in disgust.

She hated herself at that moment for being so damned incompetent. Worse, she knew that the outlaws' escape would not sit well with her boss, Marshal Canada H. Thompson. A stern but fair man, he wouldn't chide her or even mention how disappointed in her he was: he wouldn't have to. His grim, hard-eyed stare would make it all too clear how he felt.

Then a thought hit her and she gave an ugly laugh. Why was she worrying about what the marshal would think or say — or anyone else for that matter? Unless fate had a miracle planned for her, she was going to die out here, like the Wallace boys said.

The thought angered Liberty. She was no quitter and she had no intention of dying because of an inexperienced mistake. In her short but never dull life she had faced danger many times yet somehow always managed to survive. This time she assured herself, would be no different. No matter how bad things looked, she'd find a way to stay alive. She was sure of it.

She gazed about her, seeing nothing but flat scorched red dirt in all directions. Pick a direction, she told herself. Any direction! And then start walking. Who knows? Maybe, if luck was leaning her way, she might stumble upon some traveler or prospector or maybe even a water hole . . .

Deciding to keep the sun out of her eyes, she started walking west . . .

* * *

It was almost high noon. The heat from the blazing sun relentlessly burned down on her, blistering her exposed flesh and draining every last ounce of energy from her. It was so hot she could barely think. She had no idea how long she'd walked, or how far, just that she could go no farther. Even then, though, her will refused to give up. She somehow forced herself to keep stumbling along for another hundred yards or so, until, dehydrated and almost dead on her feet, she collapsed face-down on the hot, sun-baked dirt.

6

The next thing she remembered cool, life-saving water was trickling down her throat. Vision blurred, she blinked several times until eventually everything became clear and she saw a face floating above her.

She closed her eyes, knowing that she must be hallucinating, and then opened them again fully expecting the face to be gone.

It was. Nothing but cloudless blue sky stared back at her. She knew then she'd imagined it. She also realized she was lying on her back. She blinked again, her eyelids stiff and sunburned, and in a daze tried to remember where she was and what had happened to her. But her mind was blank. She licked her lips, lips that were cracked and swollen and even more painful to move than her eyelids, and just as she was about to close her eyes — the face returned and with it, more cool water came trickling down her throat.

Revived enough to remain conscious, Liberty stared fixedly at the face, realizing as she did that she'd never seen it before a few moments ago.

It was a young girl's face, more impudent than pretty and burned brown by the sun. It had a pert, upturned nose, a prematurely sad mouth shaped by hard times and boyishly short black hair that gleamed like a crow's wing.

But it was the eyes that Liberty was drawn to: large, wild and so dark she couldn't distinguish iris from pupil, they were framed by a unique double row of long black lashes that made them impossible to ignore or forget.

'W-Where am I?' she heard someone ask. She didn't recognize the voice. It sounded parched and croaked like a bullfrog, and it was several seconds before she realized it her own. Groggily, she raised herself up on her elbows and again asked where she was.

The girl, who wore a brown, sun-faded boy's shirt, ragged jeans and looked to be around fourteen, stared at her but didn't reply.

'Please,' Liberty begged. 'I must know. I . . . ' Suddenly it all came back to her in a rush, and she remembered everything that had taken place earlier.

Jarred by the memory she sat upright, noticed the canteen in the girl's hand and said: 'Let me have some of that. I haven't had any water since early this morning . . . '

The girl held the canteen to Liberty's lips. Liberty drank greedily — too greedily — only to have the girl pull the canteen away. Liberty reached for it but the girl shook her head and quickly got to her feet.

'You're right,' Liberty agreed. 'I shouldn't drink too much. Not right away.' She rose, stood there unsteadily for a moment, and then felt her head clear. The front of her blue dress was covered in sweat and sand. She brushed the sand away and for the first time noticed the saddled albino mule standing a few feet away.

'You live around here? Of course you do,' she added before the girl could answer. 'You must. No one in their right mind would be wandering around in this Godforsaken hellhole; especially someone so young.'

'I ain't so young,' the girl said. 'I ain't that much younger than you.'

'No, I . . . uh . . . can see that. Sorry. I didn't mean to offend you.'

'I don't live around here, neither.'

'No?'

'And I ain't lost or wandering around in hell, like you think.'

Liberty realized she'd made the girl angry and cursed herself for not choosing her words more carefully.

'Look,' she said, softening, 'I'm sorry for what I said. It was rude and I apologize. Can we start over again?'

The girl frowned, but remained silent.

'I'm a Deputy U.S. Marshal,' Liberty

explained. 'I don't have my badge with me because I was at a dance and . . . ' She stopped as the girl abruptly turned away. 'Wait,' Liberty called after her. 'Don't go. I want your mule.'

The girl paused, looked back and shook her head. 'It ain't for sale.'

'You don't understand,' Liberty said. 'I'm not trying to buy it. I need it to chase down two escaped outlaws.'

Ignoring her, the girl grabbed the mule's short ridge of white mane and swung up into the saddle.

Liberty hurried to her and grasped the reins, saying: 'Listen, I don't want to seem ungrateful — I mean, you saved my life — but I have to go after those men.'

The girl scowled, her dark double-lashed eyes filled with distrust. 'I don't believe you.'

'It's true,' Liberty assured her. 'I wouldn't lie to you.'

'Already have. You're no girl marshal. Ain't no such thing. You're just tryin' to steal my mule.'

'No, no, that's not true. I have to get to Okfuskee Flats. I'll pick up a horse there and then you can go on your way, I swear.'

'Let go!' the girl shouted, trying to jerk the reins out of Liberty's hands. 'Let go, I tell you!' Then as Liberty doggedly hung on: 'Damn you anyways. I should've let you die.'

'I'm grateful you didn't,' Liberty said. 'Most grateful.'

'Then why you trying to steal my mule?'

'I'm not. I just told you, I only want to borrow it.'

'Liar.'

'I'm not lying. I swear to you. Everything I've said is the Gospel truth.'

Then as the girl glared at her in angry silence:

'Tell you what. Let me ride behind you to the Flats and when I capture the Wallace brothers, I'll see you get the reward.'

'Reward?'

'It's five hundred dollars for each one, and since there's two of them that means a thousand. A thousand dollars,' she repeated, seeing the girl's wild dark eyes widen. 'Just think what you could buy with all that money.'

'You mean that?' the girl said after she'd thought about it. 'Y'ain't stringin' me along?'

'Got my word on it. The word of a Deputy U.S. Marshal.'

The girl chewed on it for another moment. 'Honor bound?'

'Honor bound,' Liberty repeated.

The girl sighed, 'Hope I don't regret this,' and grudgingly offered Liberty her hand.

'Thanks, you won't.' Liberty swung up behind her.

The girl kicked the mule with her heels and the placid animal plodded in the direction of Okfuskee Flats.

7

They had ridden for at least a mile in the glaring hot sun and the girl hadn't said a word. Liberty, though not by nature gregarious, felt sufficiently curious about her rescuer to at least find out who she was.

'My name's Liberty. Liberty Mercer. What's yours?'

'Clementina.'

'That's an unusual name.'

The girl shrugged but didn't say anything.

'Pretty, too.'

No answer.

'Don't you think so?'

'Reckon.'

They rode on, the girl so quiet that Liberty wondered if she'd offended her again.

Suddenly, the girl said: 'I used to think it was pretty.'

'What changed your mind?'

'Folks.'

'What do you mean?'

'Don't matter how many times I tell folks my name is Clementina, they still call me Clem.'

'Oh.'

The girl fell silent again and Liberty realized the conversation was over unless she continued it.

'Clem what?'

The girl hesitated, reluctant to give her surname.

'I'll need your last name if I'm to wire Guthrie for the reward money.'

'Wallace,' the girl blurted. 'My name's Clem Wallace!'

Surprised, Liberty leaned her head forward, over the girl's shoulder, saying: 'Wallace? Are you related to — ?'

'They're my brothers — well, step-brothers.'

Liberty didn't know what to say.

'You don't have to worry none,' Clem continued. 'They may be my brothers, but I hate 'em. All of 'em. I hate Ma, too. Worst of all.'

Her voice was filled with so much venom Liberty couldn't let it go.

'You surely can't mean that. Not about your own mother.'

'I do. And she ain't my real mother . . . she's my stepmother. I only call her Ma 'cause she makes me do it.'

Liberty shrugged. 'Real or not, I'd still like to know why you hate her so much.'

'She's behind it all.'

'Behind what?'

'My brothers bein' like they are. It's her fault.'

'How do you figure that?'

''Cause they all listen to her. They don't listen to nobody else, but they listen to Ma. Do whatever she tells 'em. An' she tells 'em plenty — 'specially when it comes to robbing and killing folks.'

'Your step-mother tells your brothers to rob and kill people?' Liberty said incredulously. 'Surely you must be exaggerating.'

'I ain't, believe me. Ma orders 'em around like they was toy soldiers. That's why they killed Pa,' Clem added bitterly. ' — 'cause she told 'em to.'

It was almost too much to believe. Yet Liberty sensed the girl was telling the truth.

'Why would your mother want your father killed?'

''Cause Pa wouldn't go along with her. In fact he done everything he could to stop my brothers from being outlaws. You don't have to believe me,' Clem said when Liberty looked dubious. 'But it's true. I was there. I heard Ma telling my brothers that Pa was a drunken old fool and they shouldn't listen to anything he said. And then she warned Pa to mind his own business. Said if he didn't she'd put him six feet under . . .'

'Go on.'

'That's when Pa started drinking worse than ever. I tried to stop him. First I begged him to quit an' then I kept hiding the bottles from him. But it didn't help. Somehow he always found 'em and even if he didn't, it didn't matter none 'cause Ma or my brothers would buy him plenty more. They knew that when he was liquored up he didn't try to interfere.'

'So why'd they kill him then? Why not just keep him drunk? You can tell me,' Liberty said when Clem didn't reply. 'I won't think any less of you.'

Clem sighed, her thin, shirt-covered shoulders slumping under the weight of the emotional pain she was carrying. 'One day, Ma started a-whippin' me 'cause I tried to run away. Pa, who wasn't too drunk at the time, grabbed his old scattergun and threatened Ma with it if she didn't quit beating on me. She knew he meant it, even though he was scared of her, and she quit. But she never forgave him. And a few days later, when Pa let all the horses out of the corral so my brothers couldn't ride off on a raid, Ma told Sloane — he's the oldest and meanest of all my brothers — to make sure Pa never got in their way again.'

'So it was Sloane who killed your father?'

Clem nodded.

'You actually saw him do the shooting?'

'No. Nobody did.'

'Then — ?'

'Pa just up and disappeared one night. Same night that Sloane said he was going into town — which he never done before. 'Course, Ma said not to worry about Pa — that he'd most likely gotten drunk and wandered off in the desert some place. But no one believed her. Me, least of all.'

'Anyone ever find his body or grave?'

Clem shook her head.

'So it's possible your Pa wasn't killed but decided to ride off somewhere — anywhere — rather than stay home and watch his sons turn into outlaws?'

'No, it ain't.'

'It isn't possible?'

'Uh-uh. Pa wasn't like that. He didn't have an ounce of quit in him. He'd never just take off and not come back.'

'I didn't say he would. I just said it's possible. Wouldn't you agree?'

Clem vigorously shook her head, her wild dark eyes blazing with anger.

'No. Never!'

'What makes you so sure?'

''Cause no matter what anyone says, Pa would never have run out on me. He loved me too much.'

Liberty sighed. She felt the girl's anguish and decided not to press the issue any further. Both remained silent. The all-white mule plodded on, seemingly impervious to the searing heat, the thud-thudding of its hooves and the wheezing grunt it made with each step the only sounds heard in the sun-baked wasteland.

Finally Liberty said: 'Look, I'm sorry about your father. I know from personal experience how much it hurts to lose someone you love when you're growing up.'

'Why? Did your Pa get killed too?'

'Yes — 'least I thought he did.'

'Dead's dead, ain't it?'

'That's not what I meant. I thought the man who got killed was my father, but it turned out he wasn't. I know it's confusing,' she said, seeing Clem's puzzled expression. 'But you see my mother, who was married to Pa Mercer, never told me that my real father was someone called Drifter.'

'If she never told you, how'd you find out?'

Liberty sighed, the memory distant but still painful.

'One day Comancheros attacked our ranch. They murdered my mother, Pa Mercer and both my brothers and stole all our stock. I was away at school in Las Cruces at the time and when I came home for the funeral, Drifter, this man who used to stop by our ranch every so often, told me he was my real father.'

'An' just like that, you believed him?'

'Not at first. But he knew so much about me, and my mother — personal, intimate things — that in the end I knew he was telling the truth.'

Clem mulled over Liberty's words before asking: 'What about now — is this Drifter fella still alive?'

'Yes. He raises horses on our ranch outside El Paso.'

'Why ain't you with him?'

'I was during the time I worked under Marshal Macahan in El Paso. But then I was transferred to Guthrie and . . . well, my father offered to come with me, but he loves the ranch so much I couldn't ask him sell it. Besides, I could be transferred again and then . . . ' She shrugged and let it go at that.

They rode in silence for an hour or so; then out of nowhere Clem said: 'I loved Pa more'n anything. Even when he was falling-down drunk and Ma made him sleep in the barn. Then I'd snuggle up to him and stay with him all night so nothin' bad could happen to him.'

'That was kindly of you.'

'Pa would've done the same for me. Told me so all the time. And you can believe that or not. Don't matter none to me.'

Sensing Clem wasn't finished, Liberty kept silent.

'That's why I run off.'

'From your Ma?'

Clem nodded.

'But if your father's dead — ?'

'I ain't looking for Pa,' Clem said grimly. 'I'm looking for my brothers.'

'But they're outlaws, stone-cold killers, wanted everywhere except here in Indian Territory. Surely you don't want to join up with them?'

Clem reined in the all-white, pink-eyed mule and twisted in the saddle so she could look Liberty in the face. Her eyes, black inside the frame of double lashes, blazed with hatred. And when she spoke, softer than a whisper, the same hatred filled her voice.

'I ain't looking to join up with 'em, marshal.'

'What, then?'

'I aim on killing 'em . . . all of 'em . . . for murdering Pa.'

8

If Liberty had heard that threat from a vengeful adult, she probably wouldn't have been surprised. But hearing it from a wisp of a girl — a girl not much more than a child — and with such venom caught her off-guard.

About to gently reprimand her, Liberty saw something in the girl's angry, tight-lipped expression that warned her to back off. She sensed that nothing she could say would change Clem's mind; worse, it might prod her to hate even more and then locking her up would be Liberty's only option. And it was hard to consider locking up someone who'd just saved her life!

'Look,' she said gently, 'I understand how you feel. I truly do. I'd probably feel the same way myself in your shoes. But — '

'But, what?' Clem snapped.

'Trying to kill your brothers or your mother might be harder than you think. In fact, chances are you'll most likely end up dead.'

'I don't care. Just so's they're all dead too.'

Liberty didn't say anything.

'I know what you're thinking,' Clem said. 'You're thinking it's your duty as a marshal — '

'Deputy Marshal — '

' — to stop me. Even lock me up, if you have to.'

'Did cross my mind,' Liberty admitted.

'Well, go ahead then. Won't do you no good.'

'Why's that?'

''Cause I'll just wait till you legally can't keep me locked up no longer an' have to let me go . . . and *then* I'll kill 'em.'

Seeing a lot of herself in the girl, Liberty wasn't surprised by her answer. 'Yes . . . suppose you would.'

'So you won't try and stop me then, or lock me up?'

'I can't lock you up,' Liberty said. 'Law doesn't work that way. Person has to do something wrong before they can be locked up. As for trying to stop you, that's another story. Wait,' she said as Clem started to interrupt her, 'I'm not done talking yet.'

'Don't matter. Can talk all day'n night, and there still ain't nothing you can say will make me change my mind. Nothing!'

'Maybe not. But hear me out anyway. Who knows? What I have to suggest might satisfy you without getting you killed or landing you in prison for life. That can't be all bad, can it?'

Grudgingly, Clem listened.

Liberty then explained that the two escaped outlaws she was hunting were Clem's brothers, Josh and Caleb — 'If you'll help me find them, I promise I'll arrest them and take them back to Guthrie for trial.'

'How's that gonna help me? I want

'em dead, not breaking rocks in prison.'

'Rest easy. Your brothers are wanted for murder as well as robbery. I have eyewitnesses willing to testify against them. Believe me, Clem, they won't be breaking rocks. Only future they have is dancing from a rope.'

'What if the jury finds 'em innocent?'

'There'll be no jury; just a judge. A Federal judge. Named Isaac Parker.'

'The Hanging Judge?'

'The same.'

'I heard Ma once say he only hung folks in Arkansas.'

'Not anymore. His jurisdiction now includes Indian Territory and, if need be, Oklahoma Territory too.'

'You sure 'bout that?'

'Absolutely. Few months back I was a witness myself at one of his 'neck-tie' trials. Now how about it?' Liberty said as Clem hesitated. 'Will you help me track down your brothers?'

Clem thought about it for a moment before saying: 'On one condition.'

'Shoot.'

'After you arrest Josh an' Caleb, you got to swear you'll hunt down my other brothers.'

'Be happy to — if I knew where they were holed up.'

Clem smiled. 'I know,' she gloated. 'I know where *all* their hideouts are. What's more, after you got my brothers locked up, I'll show you where Ma's cabin is. Then you can arrest her, too.'

'For what?'

'I told you: killing Pa.'

'Thought you said Sloane killed him?'

'Yeah, but on Ma's orders. That makes her to blame, don't it?'

'It could — if you can prove it. But don't forget: it's just your word against hers. The court would consider testimony like that hearsay. And even Judge Parker isn't likely to hang someone on hearsay.'

'What if we found Pa's grave?'

Liberty shrugged. 'Still be just your word against hers.'

'Not if I can make her admit to

killing him, it won't.'

'How can you do that?'

'I'll find a way,' Clem said grimly. 'And once I do, you can arrest her and make her stand trial so's Judge Parker can stretch her neck, too.'

Liberty was lost for words. She'd never heard such chilling hatred coming out of anyone — let alone a scrawny tomboy of fourteen.

9

Josh and Caleb Wallace had not ridden back to Okfuskee Flats.

Liberty searched every building, dugout, outhouse and even tent without finding them. She then questioned everyone about the Wallace brothers' whereabouts and still came up empty.

Frustrated, she was about to give up and return to Clearwater when she suddenly recalled Josh saying something about how he and Caleb planned to meet up with Sloane and the others — presumably the rest of the gang. 'If your brothers were going to get together for a meeting, you any idea where it might take place?' she asked Clem.

'Ma's cabin, maybe . . . or Coffin Rock . . . even Badwater Creek . . . I've heard 'em mention all those places at one time or another.'

'If you had to choose one, which would it be?'

'Coffin Rock.'

'Why there?'

'It's closest to here. And Sloane, he's a great one for keeping their horses fresh in case they have to run from a posse.'

'Fair enough. If I commandeer a horse, will you take me there?'

'Sure. What's commandeer mean?'

'To seize for lawful use.'

Clem arched her eyebrows. 'You can do that — steal somebody's horse and not get hung for it 'cause you're a deputy marshal?'

'It's not considered stealing,' Liberty said. 'I sign a paper that explains why I took it. It also says that the owner will get it back or another horse of comparable worth when I'm finished using it. Everything's strictly legal.'

Clem beamed, impressed. 'Stealin' horses legally. Boy, if that ain't a daisy.'

'Commandeering, not stealing,' Liberty corrected.

Clem wasn't listening. Grunting her approval, she said: 'Reckon I know what I'm gonna be when I grow up — a deputy marshal.'

'There are worse ways to make a living,' Liberty said, adding: 'C'mon. Let's get on over to the livery.'

'Why bother going there? Plenty of horses tied up outside the saloon. Take one of them, why don't you?'

'I could,' Liberty said, 'but the way I look at it, if a man's willing to pay to stall and grain his horse, most times that means he's got a fine animal and wants to take care of it — especially if he's on the wrong side of the law and might need a fast getaway.'

'Makes sense,' Clem said. 'I mean if you're gonna steal a horse, why steal a slow one?'

★　★　★

The owner of the livery stable, a disagreeable, one-legged old man named Ed Spader, didn't approve of

Liberty commandeering one of the horses stabled there. He didn't believe it was right or legal. On top of that he didn't believe she was a Deputy U.S. Marshal and backed his disbelief with an old but reliable double-barrel shotgun.

'What's more,' he said, spitting tobacco juice on the straw-covered floor, 'even if you was a lawman, like you say, you ain't no goddamn good at it, so why should I do like you say?'

'Because I'll arrest you if you don't.'

'Not so long as I'm holdin' this scattergun, you won't. All you'd be doing is runnin' your mouth — which don't surprise me none considering you're a woman.'

'Watch your tongue, old man.'

'It's true, ain't it? Hell, no lawman I ever known showed up without his badge, claiming outlaws stole his horse and his gun, and then expected me to hand over another fella's pony in exchange for a piece of written paper.'

'Damn you, you old fool,' Liberty

exclaimed. 'Every second you stand here arguing with me the Wallace brothers are getting farther away. Now put down that shotgun and — '

She broke off as Clem, who'd been inching her way around behind the old hostler, picked up a long-handled shovel and swung it hard at his head. There was a dull thud. The hostler dropped without a sound, shotgun clattering to the straw, and instantly Clem grabbed it up and aimed it at Liberty.

'All right,' she said, 'now you just stand pat, marshal, else I'll finish off what that ol' fart started.'

Liberty gaped at her. 'What're you talking about?'

'I'm going after my brothers by myself.'

'But I thought we'd agreed that my way was best all around?'

'I changed my mind.'

'Oh, for God's sake,' Liberty began.

'I'm serious, marshal. Don't take even one little step or I'll empty both barrels on you.'

'Then you'd better do it now,' Liberty said, losing her temper, 'because in two seconds I'm going to take that gun away and spank the piss out of you.'

'She means it, young'un,' a man's voice drawled above them. 'So I reckon you'd best blast away.'

Startled, both Liberty and Clem looked up and saw a bleary-eyed, stubble-faced man with long unkempt black hair watching them with droll amusement from the hay-loft.

'Go ahead,' he encouraged, 'shoot her. Like that fool hostler said 'fore you kissed him with that shovel, there ain't no such thing as a woman U.S. marshal, deputy or otherwise.' As he spoke he sat up and dangled his long legs over the edge, gun-belt in one hand and boots in the other.

'No one asked for your opinion,' Liberty said, glaring at him, 'so keep your yap shut.'

'Who are you anyways?' Clem said. 'And what's it to you whether I shoot her or not?'

'Plenty,' the man said. 'It's my horse she intends to steal.' He swung off the loft, hung there for a moment by his hands and then dropped to the floor.

Watching him, Liberty noticed that he landed squarely on his feet, catlike, and was surprised that someone who smelled and looked like a drunk was so agile.

'That a good enough reason?' the man asked Clem.

'Reckon so.'

'Well, it's not good enough for me,' Liberty said, eyeing his week-long stubble and grimy old clothes. 'You don't look like you can afford to *rent* a horse, let alone own one. And you smell like you've been sleeping in pig-slop and puked whiskey.'

'Can't dispute that,' the man said. 'My head feels like it, too.' He looked her up and down, adding: 'Looks like you could use a bath yourself.'

'What I can or can't use is none of your damn business,' Liberty snapped.

The man grinned, showing even

white teeth. 'So you can dish it out but you can't take it?'

'I don't have to take anything from the likes of you!'

'My my, touchy, ain't we?'

Liberty started to reply but Clem cut her off. 'When you two are all done acting like you was married,' she grumbled, 'maybe I can finish up my business.'

'And what business might that be?' the man inquired.

'You got a name, mister?' Liberty said before Clem could reply.

'Sure.'

'What is it?'

'Flowers. Violet Flowers.'

Clem scowled at him. 'Quit lyin', mister. Violet ain't a man's name.'

'Can't argue with you there, missy.'

'For the last time,' Liberty said, 'what's your name?'

'I just told you: Violet Flowers.' He shrugged. 'Ain't a name I would pick for myself, but since I wasn't born when it was chose for me, I didn't have no say in the matter.' He stretched and rubbed the stiffness from his back. 'Seems Ma was so set on having a girl, when I dropped out instead she got so mad she named me Violet anyway.'

'Just to spite you?'

'Reckon so.'

'My folks wanted a boy,' Clem said, the shotgun all but forgotten. 'But when the wet nurse told Pa he had a girl, he said it was God's choice and he was more'n happy to go along with it. So was my mama. But then she passed on and later, when Pa got hitched again, my step-mother didn't take to me so kindly. Fact is, she hated me from the giddyup.'

'Just 'cause you were a girl?' Violet said.

Clem nodded. 'I heard her tell my brother Lee once that if it'd been up to her, she would've drowned me like I was a three-legged kitten.'

'Woof, that's one mean-spirited woman.'

Clem, too upset by the memory to say anything, stood there in glum silence.

Feeling her pain, Violet leaned over and gently took the shotgun from her. 'Reckon we're two of a kind, missy. That makes us pals.'

'Mister, no offense, but I ain't looking to be nobody's pal.'

'Sorry to hear that,' Violet said. 'Life's already tougher than a bag of nails without a body making it tougher by going it alone.' He broke open the gun, removed the two shells and pocketed them. His movements were smooth and easy, as if he was familiar with guns, and again Liberty stored her observations away.

Meanwhile, Violet snapped the scattergun shut, leaned it against one of the stalls and buckled on his gun-belt. 'You really a Deputy U.S. Marshal?' he asked Liberty.

'Yes. And I need your horse.'

'So do I,' he said affably.

'But I'm the law.'

'So you keep saying.'

'And under special circumstances, like these, that gives me the right to lawfully take your horse — '

'There ain't no law here,' Violet reminded. 'If folks aren't happy about something they just take matters into their own hands.' He rested his hand on the Colt holstered on his hip. 'And since I wouldn't want to shoot no deputy marshal, I'd be obliged if you'd keep *your* hands off my horse. He's ugly and ain't worth much, and that's the truth, but I've gotten kind of used to him.'

'Maybe so, but I still need a horse.'

'Then I reckon you should take a look out back. There's a red roan in the corral that looks like he could run to hell and gone. So if you're dead set on stealing somebody's — '

'She ain't stealing it,' Clem interrupted. 'She's . . . uhm . . . com-man-*deering* it. Right, marshal?'

'Right.' Liberty turned back to Violet. 'If the roan checks out like you say, then you can keep your horse. But if you have a spare gun, I'll ask you to hand it over — legally, you understand.

Since you were busy eavesdropping up there' — she indicated the hay loft — 'while I was talking to the hostler, you know I had mine stolen by the Wallace brothers.'

Violet looked at her as if he couldn't believe her gall. Then he chuckled and went to a saddle draped over the stall containing a rangy, long-legged chestnut with white stockings and opened the saddlebag. 'Here,' he said, digging out a single-action Colt .45 and tossing it to her, 'you can use this.'

'Thanks.'

'I ain't giving it to you, though, legal or not,' he added, rejoining them. 'But you're welcome to use it so long as we're together.'

'Together?' Liberty said, puzzled.

'Sure,' Violet Flowers said as he headed for the door. 'Didn't I mention it? I'm ridin' along with you.'

10

Liberty was not happy to have someone as foul-smelling and disreputable-looking as Violet Flowers riding with them to Coffin Rock. But since it was the only way that he'd let her borrow his gun, and she needed a gun, she agreed on one condition: he must be legally deputized. It was only temporary she explained, and his duties would end as soon as the two Wallace brothers were captured or dead, but at least this way she would be complying with the law.

Violet said he was fine with that and started for his horse. But Liberty hadn't finished. So long as he was her deputy, she added, he had to obey her orders and comport himself like a true officer of the law.

'I'd be happy to,' he said, 'if I knew what the hell 'comport' meant.'

Liberty rolled her eyes. Having an

education, she realized, was like being punctual: it didn't mean much unless there was someone there to appreciate it. 'It means,' she said wearily, 'to behave or act like a lawman, not some bleary-eyed drunk or drifter or . . . trigger-happy gunman.'

Violet shrugged in a way that showed he was not offended by her insults. 'Reckon I can do that,' he said amiably. 'Anything else?'

'Nothing I can think of right now.' Pausing, she studied him for a moment. Despite his dirty, unkempt appearance he couldn't hide the fact that he was a tall, rugged, jut-jawed man with sun-squinted gray eyes, wide shoulders, lean hips and a hard belly. He also had a wonderful boyish smile that reminded her of a dead gunman she'd once loved. As for his personality, she had to admit he was as easy going as a warm breeze.

'Well, I can think of something,' Clem grumbled.

'What?' Violet asked.

'Wouldn't hurt none if you was to

take a bath. Either that or don't ride upwind from me. You stink worse'n hog swill.'

'She's right,' Liberty agreed. 'First creek we come to, Mr. Flowers, I suggest you jump on in and scrub yourself clean.'

'Be happy to oblige,' Violet said. He belched, his sour whiskey breath making both women recoil. 'Now, if you ladies are all done complimenting me, maybe we can saddle up and put some dust behind us.'

11

Coffin Rock was only a three hour ride from Okfuskee. With rested horses and the seemingly tireless albino mule, it should have presented no problems to any of the riders. But in the relentless sweltering heat and with the trail winding steeply up and down through treacherous rocky canyons and flat open wasteland too parched for even a cactus to grow, the ride took its toll on both animal and rider.

The rock itself, a single towering slab of sandstone carved by eons of harsh winds into the shape of an upright coffin, could be seen from miles around. Encircling it were other huge weird-shaped rocks all of which had been heaved up from the earth's bowels by a massive volcanic eruption that occurred long before dinosaurs roamed the land.

Once they were in sight of Coffin Rock, Liberty reined up in the shade of a sheer canyon wall and everyone dismounted. Taking a swallow from her canteen, she wet her neckerchief and wiped the caked saliva from the red roan's muzzle. It was a gentle, appreciative animal and gratefully nudged her with its soft velvety nose. Accustomed to her own horse's irascible behavior, she looked at the roan in disbelief. 'Why, you sweet thing you, I may keep you forever,' she whispered to it; and pouring more water into her cupped palm, let the horse drink.

Clem and Violet did the same to their mounts. Then all three sat with their backs to the wall, pulled their hats low over their faces, closed their eyes and took a well-earned rest.

They awoke just before dusk. It was cooler, though still uncomfortably warm, and overhead bats darted about, gorging themselves on swarms of insects that filled the darkening sky.

Liberty stood up, stretched the stiffness from her back and looked up at Coffin Rock. There was still no sign of the outlaws.

'This place where your brothers meet,' she said to Clem, 'have you ever been there yourself?'

'Uh-uh. But I've heard 'em talk about it enough times.'

'They ever say exactly where it was?' Violet asked.

'Yeah, in one of the caves just below the rock.'

'Facing which way?'

'Toward us.'

'That means they can see us coming,' Violet said to Liberty. 'We should stay here till dark.'

He spoke quietly, almost casually, but in a tone that suggested he was accustomed to being obeyed. Liberty stored that thought away and then nodded, as if she'd already decided to do exactly that.

'Any chance of your mother being with them?' she asked Clem.

'Uh-uh. Ma was still home when I run off, and my brothers, they'd left long afore me.'

'Could be they'll want hot food for supper,' Violet said, rising. 'Then most likely we can spot their fire.'

'Sloane's smarter than that,' Clem said. 'If they do build a fire, it'll be way in the back of the cave so you can't see it from outside.'

'What about their horses?' Liberty said. 'They must have them tethered somewhere nearby — in case they suddenly have to make a run for it, like you mentioned earlier.'

''Cording to my brothers, the cave's big enough to keep the horses inside. That's why they hole up there sometimes. They feel safe.'

'Then we'll have to smoke them out,' Violet said with authority.

Liberty looked sourly at him. 'Who gave you the reins?'

He grinned sheepishly. 'Just trying to be helpful, marshal. It's your call, naturally.'

She continued to stare suspiciously at him, as if there was something about him that didn't ring true. Then lowering her gaze, she noticed the slight bulge under his shirt, just above the rattlesnake belt holding up his Levis. It was too small and flat to be a belly gun or even one of those tiny derringers that riverboat gamblers favored, and she wondered what it could be.

'It ain't a bad idea,' Clem said, breaking the silence. ' — 'specially since Lee's afraid of fire. He ain't someone who rattles easy, but he gets spooked just by the smell of smoke. I remember once when I was a little'un, the barn caught fire and Pa yelled for everyone to grab buckets of water and we all done like he said 'cept for Lee, who was so scared he run off and hid.'

'All right, you've made your point,' Liberty said. 'But look around you. Do either of you see anything that will burn?' She gestured about them at the bleak, rocky, barren landscape. 'This isn't exactly timber country.'

'There's a ravine behind Coffin Rock,' Violet said, 'with a dry riverbed running through it. It ain't seen water longer than anyone can recall, but there's still brush and a few dead trees growing along the banks — maybe we find enough wood there to smoke 'em out.'

'Sounds like you're familiar with this area.'

'I've ridden through here a time or two,' he admitted. 'Wouldn't say I was familiar with it, though.'

Liberty studied him shrewdly. 'I hate to call a man a liar, mister, but it's time for straight talk. What exactly is your play in this, Mr. Flowers?'

Violet arched his eyebrows. 'Not sure I know what you mean, marshal.'

'Deputy Marshal,' Liberty corrected. 'And you know exactly what I mean. So let's cut out the play-acting and tell me who you are and why you're willing to risk your life by throwing in with me. And please,' she said before he could reply, 'spare me any more double talk.

You're not a drunk or a town bum, even though you've made sure you look and smell like one, and you're not riding with us because you're afraid I'll run off with your gun.'

'I'm not?'

'No. What's more, you're used to giving orders, not taking them, so my guess is you're either ex-military or a Pinkerton operative or maybe a . . . ' She paused to size him up and then, as he smiled faintly as if amused, said firmly: 'No, no, you're neither of those things. You're . . . ' Again she paused and this time she didn't continue.

'I'm what?' he said. As he spoke his whole demeanor changed. He seemed to stand straighter, taller, and despite his whiskey-breath, week-old stubble and disheveled appearance he became a man who exuded authority.

Clem, who'd been watching both Violet and Liberty, couldn't contain her curiosity any longer.

'Tell us, mister,' she begged. 'Say who you are. Please.'

Violet smiled at her and in a voice almost as educated at Liberty's, said gently: 'I work for the railroad, missy.'

''Mean you swing a hammer?'

'Not exactly.'

'He's a detective,' Liberty said as the truth hit her. 'Isn't that right, Mr. Flowers?'

'Correct.'

'What's a detective?' Clem asked.

'Someone who's paid to investigate things,' Violet explained.

'What things?'

'Trouble, mostly.'

'Oh-h . . . 'Mean like a marshal or a sheriff?'

'Sort of — except I only deal with trouble that concerns the railroad.'

Clem frowned, eyed how disreputable and filthy Violet looked, and said: 'Ain't none of my business, mister, but I reckon you should ask for a raise — then you wouldn't have to go 'round looking and stinking bad as you do.'

'You could also afford a badge,'

Liberty said. ' — maybe like the one you've got tucked under your shirt there.'

Violet acknowledged her observation with a slight grin, then turned to Clem, saying: 'I look like this so that the men I'm after won't guess who I am. It's called working undercover.'

'Oh,' Clem said.

Violet turned back to Liberty and referring to the bulge, said: 'You got a keen eye, Deputy.'

'And a good memory,' she said. 'I've heard of you, detective. You're Val Forsythe, aren't you?'

'Guilty as charged.'

'I knew it,' Clem exclaimed. 'I knew no man could be called Violet, sure as Christmas comes — 'specially when his last name is Flowers.'

Violet chuckled. 'Does seem a mite unlikely, doesn't it?' He looked at Liberty and ruefully shook his head. 'I knew I was in trouble soon as I saw you. But I was hoping you wouldn't remember.'

Liberty frowned, puzzled. 'Remember what?'

'That we'd met before.'

'We did — have — where — when?'

'New Mexico. Little town alongside the railroad — '

'Wait, wait,' Liberty interrupted. 'We met in Santa Rosa?'

'Sure. At the stock yards one morning. I was there investigating some stock that had been stolen from boxcars on the El Paso-Las Cruces line, and you, your brothers and your Pa, Fred — no, Frank — Frank Mercer were there to pick up some mares he'd bought. We were all talking to Sheriff Lonnie Forbes when you came running up and — ' Violet paused, looked at Liberty and teasingly added: 'You've grown some since then, Deputy. And if you don't mind my saying, all for the good.'

Liberty reddened. 'What do you expect? That was seven years ago. I was still at St. Marks and — '

Violet, who'd been staring at Liberty

83

as if trying to remember something that was bothering him, suddenly blurted: 'Emily! Emily Mercer. By God, I've been racking my brains trying to remember what your Pa called you — '

'Her name ain't Emily,' said Clem. 'It's Liberty. Right, marshal?'

'It is now,' Liberty said. 'But when I was growing up, it was Emily — Emily Margaret Mercer. I had it changed legally right before I pinned on the badge.'

'Why'd you go'n do that for?'

Liberty thought a moment, her mind sadly drifting back to another time, then said: 'Years ago there was this other deputy marshal, someone I really admired, and her name was Liberty. She was the first woman to ever be sworn in as a field deputy and from what Marshal Thompson told me, she had to endure all kinds of insults and threats from men who were jealous and prejudiced before she was finally accepted. I only knew her for a short time, but she was one of the most honest, straightforward people I've ever met. She never asked for or expected any special treatment or favors, just respect for doing her job, and though she would've been the last person to admit it, there's no denying that she paved the way for the rest of us women.'

'I've heard of her,' put in Violet. 'Made quite a name for herself in Indian Territory.'

'New Mexico and Texas, too,' Liberty said, adding: 'Knowing her was a real privilege and I vowed if I ever did wear a badge I'd change my name to Liberty.'

'Didn't she mind you doing that?' Clem said.

'Unfortunately, she was dead by then — gunned down by a professional bounty hunter named Rawlins.'

'Latigo Rawlins?' Violet said, surprised. 'You knew him?'

'Uh-uh. But I've sure heard plenty about him. Folks who knew him swear he was the fastest gun they ever saw

— even faster than Gabriel Moonlight or John Wesley Hardin.'

'He was also the deadliest.'

'Did he really enjoy killing, like they say?'

Liberty frowned, saddened by the thought. 'Sometimes it seemed that way. My father said it was because Latigo had no conscience or feelings, but that wasn't true. He certainly had feelings for me — strong feelings.'

'He cared about you, you mean?'

Liberty nodded. Her mind drifted back along the chains of memory. She saw Latigo's boyishly handsome face and engaging smile, a smile that belied his quick-temper and killer instinct, and remembered, regretfully, how much they had once loved each other. She'd been young then, barely sixteen and still at St. Marks, and sneaking out of the convent at night to be with Latigo had finally gotten her expelled. She'd returned home in disgrace but despite Drifter's advice to stay clear of the little Texas gunman, she'd considered running away with him. But then he'd coldly killed her friend Liberty, and her feelings toward him had changed.

'There's a rumor,' Violet was saying, 'that Rawlins was once a hired gun for Stillman J. Stadtlander, but I don't know how true it is.'

'Sadly, it's very true. But then Latigo's gun was for hire to anyone who could afford it. And Stadtlander, being the biggest cattleman in New Mexico, had enough money to hire twenty Latigos.'

'I take it you knew him, too?'

'All too well, unfortunately. He was an awful man. And his son, Slade, was worse.'

'So I've heard.' Violet thought a moment before asking: 'How about the outlaw, Gabriel Moonlight or Mesquite Jennings, as he was called?'

Liberty nodded. 'I knew Gabe, yes.'

Hiding his surprise, Violet studied Liberty shrewdly for a moment before saying: 'For someone so young and well-educated, deputy, you've led a very 'interesting' life. Some day you must tell me all about it.'

Liberty smiled mirthlessly. 'Shame on you, Mr. Flowers.'

'What d'you mean?'

'Why don't you come right out and say what you mean?'

'Thought I just did.'

'You're fishing,' she chided. 'Trying to bait me into answering a question you don't have the guts to ask.'

Clem, who'd been listening intently, scowled and shook her head. 'Wished I knew what the devil you two was carrying on about.'

Liberty again smiled without humor. 'Mr. Flowers, here, is trying to figure out how a supposedly genteel girl bent on being a lawman could possibly be friends with outlaws, professional gun-slingers and bounty hunters. Isn't that right, detective?'

'Guess I'm easy to see through, huh?'

'Like a clean window.'

He grinned sheepishly. 'I'd still like to know the answer — for strictly personal reasons, you understand.'

Liberty sighed. She'd been hoping to avoid mentioning her past, but now it seemed she had no choice; not unless she wanted it to appear that she had something to hide.

'The answer's simple. Though I was raised by the Mercers, my real father's name is Longley and he was friends with both Gabriel Moonlight and Latigo Rawlins.'

'Longley — Quint Longley — the fella known as Drifter?'

'Don't tell me you know him?'

'Some. I met him a few times when I was working alongside Marshal Macahan in El Paso. Ezra was always talking about him.'

'I don't believe it,' Liberty said. 'I worked for Marshal Macahan before I came here.'

'Small world, as they say.'

Clem scowled at them, as if betrayed, and said darkly: 'Seems to me, I'm the only person 'round here who is who she says she is.'

'Can't argue with that,' Violet said. 'And if truth be known, it gets even more complicated.'

'That ain't possible,' Clem said.

'Now's as good as any time to come clean,' Liberty told Violet.

He hesitated, inwardly cringing as he said: 'Violet Flowers *is* my real name.'

'Honest real?' Clem said.

'Honest real.' Violet grinned. 'Hell, nobody'd be fool enough to make up a gaudy handle like that.'

Clem shook her head, as if not knowing what to believe, and brushed her shiny black hair out of her eyes.

'All right,' she said finally. 'Saying I do believe you, which I ain't saying for sure, what're you doing here — *really* doing here? I mean there ain't no railroad for miles around, so — '

Liberty, who'd noticed how uneasy Violet looked, cut Clem off. 'Maybe Mr. Flowers can't tell you. Maybe it's a secret.'

'That's it,' Violet said, giving her a grateful look. 'It's a secret.'

Clem scowled. 'Grownups,' she said, disgusted. 'Why is it you always think young'uns are stupid?'

'I don't think you're stupid,' Violet began.

She stopped him. 'You're after my brothers for robbing and killing folks on your trains, mister. That's the secret, ain't it?'

'Well, I — '

'Just tell me one thing: you gonna hang 'em if you catch them?'

Violet looked uncomfortable. 'That ain't up to me, missy. That's for a judge or jury to decide. My job's just to arrest them and bring them in.'

'An' if they won't come peaceably, will you hang 'em then?'

Violet hesitated before saying uneasily: 'I'm sure it won't come to that.'

Liberty stifled a laugh. 'It's all right,' she assured him. 'You don't need to tread lightly on Clem's account. Way she feels about her brothers, she'll gladly supply the rope.'

12

As soon as dusk fell, Liberty, Violet and Clem walked their mounts around the massive base of Coffin Rock to the narrow ravine behind it. There, as Violet had mentioned, they found enough dead wood scattered about the dry riverbed to build a good fire. Cutting a length of rope from the end of his lariat Violet, with Clem's help, bound the wood into two bundles. Liberty, meanwhile, crawled to the front of Coffin Rock to see if she could spot anyone on guard outside the three caves near the summit of the base.

'They must feel pretty confident,' she said when she rejoined them. 'Haven't bothered to post a single lookout.'

'Complacency kills,' Violet said.

Liberty smiled. She was starting to like this man and was now glad she'd agreed to let him come along. 'Seems

Marshal Macahan taught you the same rules he taught me.'

'Pays to listen to experience, I always say.'

'Goodgodalmighty,' Clem said. 'You two gonna prattle on about old times all night or are we gonna burn my brothers out of that there cave?'

Liberty and Violet swapped wry looks.

'You heard the boss,' Liberty said, rising. 'Let's get to work.'

'After we set the cave on fire,' Clem said, 'let's shoot 'em as they come runnin' out. It'll save hanging them.'

'Judas, you're a blood-thirsty little soul,' Violet said. 'Where'd you learn to hate like that?'

'Wouldn't you hate someone who killed your Pa?'

'Reckon I might at that,' he admitted. Then to Liberty: 'You and missy wait here while I find out which cave they're in.'

'No need. While I was checking for lookouts, I saw smoke coming out of the middle cave. It's the largest, so it makes sense they'd hole up in it. While we're gone,' she added to Clem, 'make sure nothing spooks our horses. I've had my fill of wandering around lost and thirsty in the hot sun.'

'But I want to come with you,' Clem protested.

'Not this time.'

'But they're my brothers. I want to see they get what's coming to 'em.'

'Don't worry. You'll get your chance — right after Judge Parker sentences them. Now, do like I say or I swear I'll rope you to one of the rocks.'

Clem scowled. 'It ain't fair,' she grumbled. 'You'd be dead but for me.'

'I'm well aware of that,' Liberty said. 'And as I've already told you, I'm most grateful to you. But gratitude and wisdom are two different things. And wisdom says I need someone to guard the horses — and you're it.'

'But I don't have a gun. How am I supposed to guard anything without a gun?'

Liberty rolled her eyes. 'By guard them I meant watch them — make sure they don't run off.'

'What if wolves come? You want me to sit'n watch them while they're being eaten?'

'There are no wolves around here,' Liberty said, trying to be patient.

'How do you know? Said you'd never been here afore.'

'Oh, for God's sake,' Liberty exclaimed.

'Here, take this,' Violet tossed Clem his Winchester.

'You know how to use that?' Liberty asked her.

'Want me to show you?' Clem said belligerently.

'That won't be necessary. Just don't shoot us by mistake when we get back.'

'Without me helping you, you might never come back.'

'That's a chance we'll have to take,' Liberty said wryly. 'You ready?' she asked Violet.

He nodded:

'What about matches?'

He tapped the pocket of his shirt. 'Right here.'

'Then let's move out. The moon will duck behind those clouds soon. It'll make climbing harder, but should give us extra cover. See you in a bit,' she added to Clem.

Still sulking, Clem ignored her.

Liberty sighed wearily and picked up one of the bundles of wood. Violet grabbed the other, and the two of them started up the slope that led to the base of Coffin Rock.

Clem angrily watched them go, soon losing them in the darkening gloom. But she could still hear the sound their boots made, especially as they reached the first level of rocks supporting the base and began climbing upward.

Grumbling to herself, she sat down by her albino mule, which was tied to a dead bush alongside the two horses, leaned back and looked up at the moon. It was almost full and seemed to be grinning at her.

'Go ahead, laugh,' she told it. 'I deserve it. But just see if I ever save anybody's life again.'

13

Liberty and Violet hadn't climbed far up the rocky slope when the moon slid behind the clouds. Once its silvery brightness was gone, darkness settled in, slowing their progress.

It was a short but steep climb, made all the more dangerous by the loose shale piled between the rocks that threatened to give way at the slightest pressure. Knowing that one misstep would not only send them tumbling but alert the outlaws, they were forced to tread very carefully. As they climbed higher the angle of the rocks steepened. Their breathing became labored. Soon they needed both hands to help pull themselves up over the rocks.

Stopping on a ledge, they cut two short lengths from Violet's lariat which he'd slung over his shoulders at the start of the climb, and tied them to the bundles of wood. The bundles made a light scratching sound as they dragged behind Liberty and Violet — pausing, they looked uneasily at each other, both wondering if the noise would betray their presence. Then Violet shrugged as if to say that they had no other choice if they wanted to burn the Wallace gang out of the cave and Liberty nodded in agreement. With Violet leading, they slowly continued upward until they reached another narrow ledge right below the caves. Here they stopped to regain their wind, both crouching down so their heads didn't show above the rocks.

'One thing's for sure,' Liberty whispered, 'Clem was wrong about her brothers keeping their horses with them. They'd have to be part mountain goat to climb up here.'

'Unless there's another entrance to the cave,' Violet said. ' — a back trail for instance that's hidden by rocks or comes up through another canyon.'

Liberty scowled, irked at herself.

'Damn. I should've thought of that before. Would've saved us a lot of time and effort.'

'Take it easy. I didn't say there was another canyon — just that there might be. Anyways, a person can't think of everything.'

'Marshal Thompson would've thought of it. So would Marshal Macahan. Especially Ezra. You know how much emphasis he placed upon preparation.'

'Don't be so hard on yourself — '

'Why not? Because I'm a woman and women aren't supposed to be able to think outside the kitchen?'

Though she spoke barely above a whisper, it was through gritted teeth and Violet could tell she was furious with herself.

'No,' he said gently. ' — because those two gents have had a lifetime of experience as marshals. They've worn a badge longer than you've been born, and in that time they've come to know that success and failure go hand-in-hand.'

'You're just saying that to make me feel better — '

'No, I'm saying it 'cause it's true. I've been with the railroad almost fifteen years and I'd hate to tell you how many times I've screwed up.'

'That's not what I've heard. You've got a reputation for getting the job done.'

'Don't believe everything you hear.'

'I don't. But this was in Guthrie's *Daily State Capitol*.'

'Or read, either.'

'Now you're being modest.'

He ignored her, saying: 'Back to what we were talking about. If there is another way out, we're going to have to move fast once we start the fire or else they'll duck out the back — ' Hearing something he stopped and quickly thumbed at the caves above them.

Listening, Liberty heard footsteps approaching in the middle cave. Someone was coming out. She crouched lower and reached for the Colt .45 tucked in her belt.

Beside her Violet did the same, his hand gripping the butt of his holstered six-gun as he looked upward.

The steps grew louder and shortly a shadowy figure appeared in the mouth of the cave. They couldn't make out his face in the darkness but both saw the Winchester he was holding, cocked and ready before him.

'Can't see nobody,' he called back over his shoulder. 'Must've been the wind or some rocks falling.' After a little, he quit peering about him and returned inside. As he did, a horse whinnied in the cave and stirred restlessly. Other horses stirred with it, their hooves clattering on the rock floor — and moments later a man spoke soothingly to them, trying to calm them down.

All but one of the horses obeyed. The man started to speak to the horse and then jumped back, cursing as it tried to kick him.

'Damn you!' they heard him say. 'You try that again and I'll put a bullet in that dumb brain of yourn.'

Outside on the ledge Liberty grinned and whispered to Violet: 'Bet that's Regret.'

'Your horse?'

She nodded. 'Serve 'em right for stealing him.' Pausing, she then pointed to his shirt pocket. He nodded, dug out two matches and gave one to Liberty. He went to strike his on the rock but she quickly signaled for him not to; then as he paused, frowning, she sucked her forefinger and held it up to test the breeze.

Violet nodded appreciatively, whispered: 'Caution's the way, amigo.'

Liberty smiled as she heard Marshal Ezra Macahan's favorite phrase. Then leaning forward, she cupped both hands around Violet's match as he carefully scratched it on the rock. The match flared, its flame fluttering briefly inside her cupped hands, and then grew steady. Violet winked at her and together they lowered the match to his bundle of wood.

The smaller twigs caught fire almost immediately. Liberty quickly held her bundle in the flames, the dead wood instantly bursting alight. Soon both bundles were burning brightly and at Liberty's nod, Violet hurled his into the cave. Moments later Liberty threw her bundle after it.

At once they heard surprised, angry shouts, followed by cursing as men sprang up to avoid getting burned. The horses whinnied with fear and jerked free from the tether line, bringing more cursing from the outlaws.

Liberty and Violet waited no longer. Guns drawn, they scrambled over the last few rocks and charged into the large cathedral-shaped cave. It was filled with smoke and flames. At the rear, in front of a natural doorway just wide enough for a horse to squeeze through, Liberty could see the shadowy figures of the five outlaws as they fought to control their panicked horses. Motioning for Violet to follow, she closed in on the men, ready to shoot anyone who posed a threat.

When she was within ten paces of them, one of the outlaws spotted her and gave a surprised yell that alerted the others. Horses forgotten, they whirled and faced her and Violet and went for their guns.

Liberty fired a quick shot at their feet before the outlaws cleared leather. 'That's better,' she said as they froze in mid-draw. 'Now, unbuckle those gun-belts and step back.'

'Eeeasy,' Violet said as the outlaws grudgingly obeyed. 'I ain't as kind-hearted as the marshal. One of you even breathes wrong, I'll cut him down.'

The five men dropped their gun-belts and stepped back. The two bundles of wood had almost burned themselves out. Much of the smoke had escaped out the rear exit and the horses, calmer now but still trembling, stood huddled together behind the outlaws.

Recognizing Liberty, Caleb Wallace

looked at his brother and spat disgust-edly into the glowing embers of their camp fire. 'I told you we should've killed that bitch when we had the chance.'

'Always a next time,' Josh said.

'Don't count on it,' Liberty said. Then to Violet: 'Get their hardware.'

Violet obeyed, and returned beside her with five gun-belts draped over his forearm. As he did, Caleb reached for the hunting knife sheathed at his side.

Liberty snapped off a shot and Caleb yelped as the bullet punched a hole in his hand. The knife clattered to the ground, the cave echoing with the loud boom made by the shot. The horses shied nervously and one of them reared, neighing shrilly.

For an instant Liberty's gaze wan-dered to the skittish horse, knowing even before she actually saw it that it was Regret — and in that instant one of the outlaws, a short, slender man no more than twenty, reached inside his shirt and pulled out a short-barreled belly gun.

Violet shot him before he could pull the trigger. The young man dropped the gun and staggered back, both hands clutching the wound in his chest, and collapsed on the ground. There he coughed blood twice and died.

'Maybe now you'll listen to me,' Violet said to the other outlaws. 'This isn't a pretend Wild West show and I ain't Buffalo Bill.'

Liberty, after a pitying look at the dead young outlaw, wagged her gun at Josh. 'Bind up your brother's hand,' she told him. 'And be quick about it.'

Using his kerchief, he obeyed.

'No matter how long it takes,' Caleb hissed at her, 'one day I'm gonna cut your heart out.'

Liberty ignored him. 'Turn around . . . all of you,' she told the outlaws. As they reluctantly obeyed, she asked Violet fot his lariat. He slipped it off his shoulders and handed it to her, gun trained on the four men.

Liberty cut off four pieces of rope and used them to tie the outlaws' hands behind their backs. When she was finished, she herded them out the rear exit while behind her Violet followed with the horses.

14

The narrow winding trail descended between rocky hills and giant boulders that hid it from the ravine below. It took them a while to reach the bottom and by the time they did the moon had reappeared from behind the clouds. By its light Liberty saw the same dry riverbed snaked out before her and realized they weren't far from where they had earlier gathered the dead wood.

Ordering the four outlaws to keep walking, she fell back beside Violet who was still leading the horses.

'Damn this horse of yours,' he grumbled. 'It's tried to bite me twice.'

Liberty gave the buckskin an ugly look. 'Can't you mind your manners for a moment?'

The buckskin snorted, wrinkled its lips to show its big yellow teeth and gave a rebellious little buck.

'Don't take it personally,' Liberty said to Violet. 'Regret does the same to me whenever he gets the chance. He also cow-kicks, as that man found out earlier, so don't stand too close behind him.'

Violet looked at the buckskin and shook his head. 'Why do you keep the sonofabitch then? Sure ain't on account of his looks.'

'He can run to the moon and back if he has to.'

Together they followed the riverbed as it led back to the place where they'd left Clem. It didn't take long. Almost before they realized they rounded a blind curve and Liberty spotted the albino mule and their horses about twenty yards ahead of them.

Ordering the outlaws to stop, she turned to Violet, saying: 'Stay here. I want to talk to Clem before she gets any ideas about shooting her brothers.' She hurried ahead before he could argue, and soon was close enough to see Clem huddled against the sandy bank, sound asleep.

At least, that's what she thought. But as she got closer, Clem suddenly rolled over and Liberty found herself staring down the barrel of a Winchester.

'Whoa, whoa, take it easy, girl . . . it's me, Liberty . . . '

'Don't move,' Clem said, rising and keeping the rifle trained on Liberty. 'I don't want to have to shoot you.'

'What're you talking about?' Liberty said. 'Quit pointing that darn rifle at me or I'll use it to paddle you with.'

'No need for that,' Violet said, approaching with the outlaws. 'She's just running a bluff.'

'Get back!' Clem warned. 'I ain't foolin', Mr. Flowers. My brothers have got to pay for what they done to Pa.'

'Then go ahead and shoot,' Violet said. 'Here, I'll make it easy for you.' He pressed his belly against the barrel of the Winchester. 'All you got to do is pull the trigger, missy.'

Clem gritted her teeth and started to

pull the trigger — then suddenly she burst into tears, threw the rifle to the ground and ran off into the darkness.

'That was a damn fool thing to do,' Liberty chided, picking up the rifle and handing to Violet. 'The hate she's got for her kin, she just might have blown a hole through you.'

Violet grinned, pointed the rifle skyward and pulled the trigger. There was a click as the hammer struck air.

'I might've known,' Liberty grumbled. 'Anyone who learned his ABCs from Ezra Macahan wouldn't risk his life on the whim of a vengeful child.'

'Cut me loose an' give *me* that damn rifle,' said Josh Wallace, 'see if I let you off so easy.'

Violet's flint-gray eyes narrowed menacingly. 'Oblige the man,' he told Liberty.

'What?'

'Oblige the man.'

She frowned, hesitated for a moment and then walked behind Josh and untied his hands.

Violet, meanwhile, dug a cartridge out of his pocket, chambered it, and threw the rifle at Josh's feet.

'All right, make your play.' He dropped his hand to his holstered Colt, ready to draw.

Josh looked at the Winchester lying so temptingly close at his feet and then back at Violet.

'What's wrong?' the railroad detective mocked. 'Lose your guts all of a sudden?'

Josh Wallace chewed his lip, face white with fury.

'Yellow to the bone,' Liberty scoffed.

'Seems like,' Violet said. 'But let's give him the benefit of the doubt.' He smiled thinly at Josh. 'Your call.'

Josh tensed as if slapped, but made no attempt to go for the rifle.

'Forget it,' Liberty said. 'There'll be snow on your temples before this weasel grows a spine.'

'Do it, Josh,' Caleb urged his brother. 'Do it! Go on. Pick it up and shoot the sonofabitch!'

'What're you waiting for?' Violet said to Josh. 'Not going to let your little brother down, are you?'

'Please, Josh, shoot him,' Caleb begged. '*Shoot* the no-good bastard!'

Josh twitched with rage, but didn't move.

'Figures.' Violet shook his head in disgust and then looked in the direction of where Clem had run off. 'I know you're watching, missy,' he called out. 'I was just trying to prove a point. Show you why there's no need to waste time hating your brothers. Pity 'em, maybe, but, believe me, they're too pathetic to hate.'

'Damn you to hell,' raged Josh.

'It's most likely where I'll end up,' Violet said, 'but not on account of you.' He turned his back on Josh and called out: 'Clem . . . ? Clem, you can come on in now.'

'Do as he says,' Liberty shouted. 'It's time we got this trash over to Clearwater.'

Slowly, Clem appeared out of the darkness. Hate still blazed in her dark

114

eyes but it was a controllable hate and Liberty knew that she wouldn't cause any more trouble.

'Go tie up your brother's hands,' she said, handing Clem the rope. 'And make sure the knots are tight.'

Both Josh and Caleb glared at Clem as she approached.

'Best think twice 'fore you listen to her,' Josh warned.

'Better hope I don't,' Clem replied bitterly. ''Cause if I get to thinking, I'll get filled with hate again and shoot you.'

'When Ma finds out what you done,' Caleb said, 'she's gonna beat you bloody.'

'She'll have to find me first,' Clem said as she tied his hands behind his back. ''Cause I sure as rotten eggs ain't going home no more.'

'Don't matter. You won't be hard to find,' Josh said. 'Me'n Caleb will track you down easy.'

'I wouldn't bet on that,' Liberty said. 'Not unless you know of a way to talk

115

Judge Parker out of stringing you up.'

'He may hang us,' Caleb said, trying to sound tough. 'But that won't stop Sloane or Lee or Virge from finding her.'

'Yeah,' Josh said. 'And when they do, little sister, they'll drag you back home and whip the skin off your back.'

'Wouldn't be the first time,' Clem said defiantly. 'And I'm still here, ain't I?' Finished tying his hands, she picked up a rock at her feet and before anyone could stop her, clubbed him on the back of the head. Josh staggered forward and dropped to his knees, stunned, blood coming from his head.

Clem, seeing Liberty and Violet's surprised looks, said: 'You told me I couldn't kill 'em. Never said I couldn't beat on 'em.'

'True enough,' Liberty admitted. 'But don't make a habit of it or else your brothers won't be in condition to stand trial.' Turning to Violet, she added: 'Help those boys back on their horses and let's make some dust.'

15

It was almost noon the next day when they entered Clearwater.

With Liberty leading the four outlaws, and Violet and Clem bringing up the rear, they rode down the middle of Front Street, half in and half out of the shadows cast by the double-row of false-fronted, sun-bleached buildings.

Everywhere people stopped what they were doing and stared at the grim little party. Word of the outlaws' capture quickly spread. Soon storekeepers, bartenders, saloon girls, blacksmith and hostler, even businessmen came out to join them, their faces a mixture of surprise and curiosity as they recognized the two infamous Wallace brothers.

Even the big white dog, Trouble, stopped urinating on a corral fence still covered with election posters to watch them ride past.

Reining up outside the marshal's office, Liberty dismounted, tied up her horse and told Violet to help the outlaws off their mounts. She then turned to Clem, who'd slid down from her saddle, and thumbed at the office, saying: 'Tell the sheriff to come on out.'

Clem nodded and ran into the office. Moments later she reappeared, followed by a short, powerfully built man in a brown suit, white shirt and a black string tie who walked unsteadily and looked pale and sickly.

'Got some guests for you, Will,' Liberty said.

'So I see,' Sheriff Hagen said. He pushed his Stetson back from his forehead and wiped his sleeve across his sweaty brow. 'Be obliged if you'd stick around till they're behind bars. This fever's left me a little shaky.'

Liberty nodded and signaled to the outlaws. 'Step down, gentlemen, and I'll introduce you to your new home. But don't get too comfortable,' she warned as they obeyed. 'Like I told you,

118

we'll be heading to Guthrie first thing in the morning.'

She herded the prisoners toward the office. The crowd that had gathered nearby, both in the street and on the awning-covered boardwalk, now eagerly surged forward to get a better look at the outlaws.

'That's close enough,' Sheriff Hagen told them. 'That includes you,' he added to Violet and Clem.

'They're with me,' Liberty said. She turned to Violet. 'Be grateful if you'd take Clem to the hotel and get her a room and maybe a bite to eat. I'll be with you soon as I'm done here.'

'Sure thing.'

'Oh, and tell Tom Akins at the front desk to charge her keep to the marshal's office.'

'Be happy to. C'mon,' Violet said to Clem. 'Let's go get ourselves cleaned up and afterward, find somewhere to get some grub.'

She ignored him. She stood there, glumly watching as Liberty and Sheriff

Hagen escorted the outlaws into the office. 'They're gonna need a stronger jail,' she muttered. 'Either that or a quick hanging.'

'What're you talking about?' Violet said. When she didn't reply, he grasped her by the shoulders and forced her to look at him. 'Do you know something Liberty and I don't?'

'I know my brothers,' Clem said, 'an' that's all I need to know.'

'That doesn't answer my question. Now spit it out.'

'Sloane will never let Josh an' Caleb hang. Neither will Virge or Lee.'

'Maybe they won't hear about it till it's too late?'

'They'll hear.'

'You think news of their arrest will travel that fast? They only just got locked up and you heard what Liberty said: she's taking them to Guthrie first thing in the morning.'

'Don't matter,' Clem said grimly. 'They got ears everywhere — and most of 'em friendly.' She paused and shading her eyes, looked off up the sun-baked dirt street. 'Like as not, somebody's rid off to tell 'em already. It's like Ma always says,' she added disgustedly, ' — gold talks, justice walks.'

Violet couldn't argue with that. Taking Clem's arm, he led her across the street to the Hotel Independence.

'What's going to happen to me, Mr. Flowers?' she asked as they stepped onto the boardwalk fronting the two-story, red-brick hotel. 'After we get washed up, I mean?'

'I told you: we'll get ourselves the best grub we can find.'

'And after that?'

'We'll worry about that when the time comes.'

'I meant it when I said I ain't going back to live with Ma. I'd sooner die first.'

'Don't worry. I'd look after you myself before I'd let that happen.'

'Promise?'

'Got my hand on it,' he said, offering her his hand.

She grasped it eagerly, as if she couldn't believe her luck, and shook hands.

'All right,' he said. 'Now, let's quit jawing and go get ourselves prettied up. I'm kind of curious to see how you look under all that dirt and dust.'

'No different,' she said. ' — 'cept cleaner.'

They entered the hotel.

16

It was around one o'clock when Liberty joined them in the well-appointed, wood-paneled hotel dining room. She had cleaned up and changed clothes at her house, and now wore her customary sun-faded Levi's, blue denim shirt, rough-out boots and a Colt .44 with a hair-trigger holstered on her right hip. She also had her Deputy U.S. Marshal's badge pinned to her shirt.

'Hell, you didn't need to get all gussied up for my benefit,' Violet said as she joined him and Clem at a table by the window. 'If I'd known that was your intention, I would've worn my Sunday-go-to-prayers suit.'

'Ignore him,' Clem told Liberty. 'You look just fine to me, marshal.'

'Thanks. 'Least my feet don't hurt in those catalogue pinch-toe shoes any more.' Liberty paused and smiled at

Clem, who though clean was still wearing her trail-worn clothes. 'I was thinking,' she continued. 'After we get through eating, we'll go to Greenwood's. A shipment of new clothes came in from St. Louis just before the election, and I seem to remember seeing a whole parcel of things that would fit you.'

'Thanks, but I don't need no charity,' Clem said quickly.

'It's not charity. I'll charge everything to the marshal's office.'

'I don't need no new clothes, neither.'

'Sure you do,' Liberty said. 'You've got a thousand dollars coming to you soon.'

'A thousand dollars?' Violet gave a low whistle. He'd shaved, brushed his long dark hair back and put on a fresh shirt. Though creased from being in his saddle-bags, it fitted him well. His shoulders looked even wider and his hips leaner. It was also the same steel-gray as his eyes and Liberty, as if seeing him for the first time, was surprised at how attractive he was.

'It's the reward money,' she explained, 'for leading to the capture of the Wallace brothers.'

'Boy, that's a mighty impressive sum of money.'

'Indeed it is,' Liberty said. 'And because of that, Clem, a lot of folks around here are going to be scrutinizing you — '

'Scrutin-what?' Clem said.

'Watching you and talking about you. Surely that's reason enough to buy some new finery.'

'I don't want the reward,' Clem said sullenly. 'Ain't nothin' but blood money.'

'Where'd you get that idea from?'

'Sheriff Hagen. I heard him say it while you were taking my brothers into his office.'

'Don't listen to him. Will's just jealous he isn't getting any of it.'

'Don't matter. I don't want it. I wouldn't know what to do with all that money, anyways.'

'How about paying for your schooling?' Violet suggested.

'I hate school,' snorted Clem.

'Everybody hates school,' said Liberty. 'It's part of growing up. But you still have to go.'

'Why?'

''Cause you want to be a marshal one day, don't you? 'Least, that's what you said and I believed you. And you can't be a marshal or even a deputy marshal if you don't have any schooling.'

'Maybe I'll be a railroad detective instead,' Clem said, eyeing Violet. 'They don't have to go to school, do they?'

''Fraid so, missy. So if that's what you want to be — or a marshal — you're just going to have to take the money. It's yours anyway. You earned it. Without you, Josh and Caleb and those other two men would still be riding around shooting and robbing folks. That's not what you want, is it?'

'Reckon not.'

'And neither did your Pa,' reminded

Liberty. 'Don't forget him and all he tried to do for your brothers.'

'I ain't forgetting,' Clem said sadly. 'I'll never forget Pa. It's just my mind's all mixed up trying to figure out what's right from wrong. I mean, truth is I just want to see my brothers get what's coming to 'em. That's all.'

'I thought we'd already settled that?' Liberty said. 'I've already wired Judge Parker. Told him that I'm bringing your brothers and two other members of the Wallace gang in to Guthrie tomorrow. It'll just be a matter of days before they stand trial.'

There was a heavy silence as Clem stared glumly out the window at the townspeople passing by.

Liberty gave Violet a puzzled look. 'Is something wrong? Have you two quarreled or something?'

'Nope.'

'Then why the long face?'

'Clem doesn't think either Josh or Caleb will ever *stand* trial — in fact, she figures you won't even get them on the train tomorrow.'

'That's ridiculous. Why not?'

''Cause my other brothers are going to bust them out,' Clem blurted. 'An' neither you nor the sheriff nor nobody else will be able to stop 'em — that's why not, marshal!'

Liberty shot Violet a look. 'You know anything about this?'

'Just what she told me.'

Liberty turned to Clem. 'You just guessing or do you know for sure they're coming here?'

'I know for sure,' Clem said grimly.

'How?'

''Cause Caleb is Ma's favorite. Always has been. So even if my brothers didn't want to bust him and Josh out, Ma would make 'em do it.'

'They're grown men,' Violet said. 'Surely they're past being bullied into doing things by their mother?'

Clem gave a bitter laugh. 'You don't know Ma, Mr. Flowers. If she set her mind to it, she could make the devil hisself come to heel.'

There was another silence, save for the chatter of other guests eating in the dining room. Then Clem said: 'And after they've broken Caleb and Josh out, they'll come looking for me.'

'To take you back home, you mean?'

Clem nodded. 'Where Ma'll be waiting with her whip.'

'That settles it,' Liberty said. 'There's only one thing to do.'

'If you're thinking of hiding me or sneaking me out of town, forget it. Sloane will hunt me down, no matter where I am.'

'I don't think Deputy Mercer was thinking of either of those things,' Violet said, reading Liberty's expression.

Clem looked at Liberty. 'You weren't?'

'Quite the opposite. I was thinking of making it easy for them to find you.'

'With my help, of course?' Violet said.

'Naturally,' Liberty said.

'I don't understand,' Clem said.

'You will,' Violet assured her. He grinned at Liberty, adding: 'Reckon that means I'm still sworn in.'

'Definitely.'

Violet winked broadly at Clem. 'Do you think it's time I made her give me a badge?'

Instead of laughing, as he'd expected, Clem looked dismayed. 'I wish you two'd be serious. You get in the way of Sloane or any of my brothers and they'll gun you down and laugh about it.'

Violet fondly pressed his hand over Clem's. 'I appreciate the warning, missy, and I'm sure the marshal here does too. And believe me, we *are* taking your brothers seriously. Very seriously.'

'Count on it,' Liberty said tersely. 'Making light of trouble, pretending it doesn't bother us, that's just our way of whistling 'round tombstones.'

Then as Clem looked relieved:

'But I am going to need your help — if you're up to it.'

'Just tell me what you want me to do.'

'Good girl.'

17

After lunch Liberty, Violet and Clem left the hotel and crossed over to the sheriff's office. It was oven-hot and flies tortured the tethered horses. There were very few wagons and riders about and those that were moved sleepily up the street. All seemed calm and peaceful until suddenly, just as a buckboard crossed in front of them, Clem darted away.

For a moment Liberty and Violet appeared to be caught off-guard. Then both yelled for Clem to stop. When she ignored them and continued sprinting on up the street, Liberty pulled her Colt and fired a warning shot that kicked up the dirt near Clem's feet.

'Hold it!' she yelled. 'Get back here or the next shot won't miss.'

Grudgingly, Clem pulled up, turned and glared at Liberty and Violet, then sullenly came walking back toward them. By now everyone on Front Street had stopped what they were doing and stood watching as she trudged past.

In a voice that she made sure was loud enough to be heard by everybody, Liberty scolded Clem for trying to run away and ordered her to get inside the sheriff's office.

'Why, I ain't done nothin',' Clem protested. 'You got no right to keep me here.'

'Wrong,' Liberty said. She tapped the badge on her shirt. 'This gives me the legal right to do whatever I want. Now quit sassing me and get inside with your brothers!'

Grudgingly, Clem obeyed.

Liberty turned and addressed the onlookers: 'Show's over, folks. Get back to what you were doing.' She stood there, thumbs tucked in her gun-belt, looking fixedly at everyone until reluctantly they obeyed.

As she went to enter the office, she noticed Trouble plodding toward her.

The great white dog was limping and there was blood on its left front paw.

Liberty hunkered down in front of it. 'What's wrong, boy? Step on a thorn or something?'

The dog stopped, bared its fangs and uttered a low rumbling growl.

Liberty shrugged and straightened up. 'Suit yourself. I was just going to take a look and see if I could help.' She entered the office.

Trouble paused in front of the door, its dark-brown eyes staring after Liberty, and then limped off.

Inside, Liberty joined Violet and Clem at the window. 'That ought to do the trick,' she said as they watched the townspeople dispersing. 'If your brothers do have anyone spying on us, that little act of ours should convince them that you're spending the night behind bars.'

The door burst open and Sheriff Hagen came bustling in. He was sweating and winded from running, and not waiting to catch his breath he demanded to know what was going on — 'Ed over to the barbershop says you actually took a shot at this young'un?' he added before Liberty could answer. 'That true, deputy?'

'Damn right it's true. She's lucky I didn't wing her.'

'She took off running,' Violet explained to the sheriff. 'Had her mind set on telling her other brothers that Josh and Caleb were locked up, and due to be taken to Guthrie on the morning train — '

'I already wired Judge Parker about bringing them in,' Liberty said. 'I also told him that I hoped to get a fast trial and an even faster hanging.'

'And if those charges aren't enough to earn them a rope,' Violet added, 'I've been hunting them for weeks for shooting two guards while robbing an AT&SF train outside Coffeyville, Kansas — '

Sheriff Hagen frowned, surprised. 'You're a railroad detective?'

'He sure is,' Clem blurted. 'What's

more, he's trying to 'railroad' my brothers. An' it ain't right. Much as I hate 'em, they deserve a fair trial just like anybody else.'

'Oh, it'll be fair,' Violet assured her. ' — all the way to the gallows.'

'Well now, just hold on a minute,' Sheriff Hagen said. 'Maybe she — '

Liberty cut him off. 'Lock the brat up, Will. And don't let her out till I say so.'

Sheriff Hagen paled at the idea of crossing the Wallace brothers. 'Y-You lock her up, marshal. I'm getting my fever back. Reckon I'll head on home and rest up a spell.'

'Come to think of it,' Liberty said, peering at him, 'you do look a bit poorly.'

She waited till the sheriff had hurried out, then she grabbed the cell keys off the hook on the wall and joined Violet and Clem at the window. The three of them watched as the lawman mounted and spurred his horse out of town.

'You figure he's truly sick,' Violet said, 'or just using that as an excuse so he can get a message to Clem's brothers?'

Liberty shrugged. 'Hard to tell. There's some in town say he coils when he sits, but I've never had reason to doubt his honesty.'

'What're you gonna do with me now?' Clem asked.

'Sneak you out the back door and then Mr. Flowers, here, will make sure you get to the Neilson place safely.'

'I will?' Violet said, surprised.

Liberty continued as if he hadn't spoken. 'Then if your brothers do ride in and try to break Caleb and Josh out, you'll be out of harm's way.'

'But what about you?' Clem said anxiously. 'You can't hold my brothers off by yourself.'

'I don't intend to,' Liberty said. 'By then I'll have sworn in a posse and we'll be waiting for them.'

'And I'll be right beside you,' Violet said. 'I don't intend to play mother hen

136

— no offense, Clem — and miss all the fireworks.'

'So long as you're my deputy,' Liberty said, 'you'll follow my orders. And my orders are that you stick with Clem and make sure nothing bad happens to her.'

'And if I refuse?'

'I'll toss you in jail too — for dereliction of duty.'

Violet glared at Liberty. Then, 'You're my witness,' he said to Clem. With that, he removed an imaginary badge from his shirt and pretended to set it on the desk before Liberty.

'What're you doing?'

'Resigning . . . as of right now.'

Liberty smiled as if she'd just found gold. 'Figured you'd say that,' she said. Taking a piece of paper from her pocket, she set it on the table before Violet. 'That's why I wired your boss. Sympathetic gentleman, Mr. Hiram. Understood my problem at once. Said he was putting you under my command for as long I wanted.'

Violet looked at her, first in surprise, then in disbelief; then he grabbed the wire and read it. As if still not believing what it stated, he read it again. Then he slammed it down on the desk and glared defiantly at Liberty.

'He forgot to mention one very important fact.'

'What might that be, Deputy Flowers?'

'That I was no longer working for him . . . or the railroad.'

Now it was Liberty who looked surprised. 'Since when?'

'Since you started ramrodding me around.' He bent over and fondly kissed Clem on the top of her head. 'Been a pleasure, Miss Clementina. Hope I meet up with you again sometime.'

'W-Wait. Where you going?'

'Anywhere but here.' He tipped his hat politely at Liberty, 'Deputy,' and walked out.

'Be damned,' she said.

'Well?' Clem said to her as Liberty remained standing there.

'Well, what?'

'Ain't you gonna go after him and apologize?'

'When the fires of hell burn out.'

'Be sorry if you don't.'

'Ha!' Liberty snorted. 'You've got a lot to learn about being a woman.'

'Maybe,' Clem said, 'but I ain't the one who's eating his dust. Nor the one who's already regretting it 'cause she knows how much she needs him.'

Liberty started to berate her, changed her mind and glared out the window after Violet. Then, teeth gritted, she said something unflattering about men in general and slammed out the door.

Clem went to the window and watched as Liberty caught up with Violet farther along the boardwalk. There was a brief heated conversation between them, with Liberty doing most of the talking. Then as Violet shrugged and started to walk on, she grudgingly said something that made him turn around and walk back to her. He was smirking like he'd struck pay dirt. Furious, she spun around and stormed back to the office, Violet strolling along behind her.

Clem turned from the window as Liberty entered. 'There — was that so hard?'

'Hardest damn' thing I've ever done in my life.'

'But worth it.'

Liberty started to say no, but then she looked at those incredibly dark-lashed eyes staring up at her and all her anger faded.

'Yes,' she admitted wryly. 'Well worth it.' Resting her hands on Clem's bony shoulders, Liberty kissed her fondly on the forehead. 'Thanks for the advice, young lady. Reckon we all need our brains straightened out once in a while.'

'It wasn't just for you,' Clem said as Violet came through the door. 'I need him too.'

18

The rest of the day dragged on. There was no sign of the Wallace gang but with each passing hour the townspeople grew more tense and afraid, and by sundown the streets were empty and all the stores were closed.

But there were plenty of faces peering out the various windows, everyone fearful of what was going to happen if and when the Wallace gang showed up.

Earlier, Liberty had called a meeting at the town hall. She'd only invited the men, hoping that she could find enough volunteers among them to help her drive off the outlaws. But only a handful of men showed up and none of those seemed anxious to face the dreaded Wallace brothers — especially if she was leading them.

'My advice to you,' Mayor Justin told

Liberty, 'is to drop all the charges against the boys you got in jail and send them packing. Maybe then, if it ain't already too late, Sloane and the rest of the gang won't bother riding in here after our blood.'

Liberty gave him a withering look. 'Bob,' she said slowly, 'I'm willing to overlook that you're a pompous, selfish blowhard, and so are most other folks around here — they showed that by voting for you. But voting for a man to be mayor, an office that no one else wanted in the first place is one thing; having a mayor who's a liar and a damn' coward to boot, a man who'd sell his soul and everyone else's along with it just so he doesn't have to stand up for what he knows is right, what is the *law* — well, that's another thing entirely. And I, for one, will make sure everyone in the Territory hears about it.'

Mayor Justin erupted. 'Goddamn you, deputy! You got no call to talk to me like that. What I'm proposing ain't cowardly, it's common sense.' He included the other men around him as he added: 'Just 'cause we all know how to shoot a gun doesn't make us gunmen. If we try to stand up to these outlaws like you're proposing, we'll all die. That's a certainty. And knowing Sloane Wallace, who's mean as a rattler, he and his men won't be content with just killing us. They'll most likely murder our women and children too — just for the pure fun of it.'

A murmur of agreement came from the other men.

'I won't deny that it's dangerous,' Liberty said. 'But what you're all forgetting is he may do that anyway — on orders from his Ma, just because I locked up Josh and Caleb.'

'Maybe, maybe not,' put in Walt Neuhauser. 'Hopefully the fact that we released them without doing them harm will make a difference. Even a man evil as Sloane Wallace knows if he guns us down, he'll have the governor and every lawman in the territory hunting him, all wanting to stretch his neck. That's got to count for something in our favor.'

'Walt's right,' Tom Akins, the hotel clerk said to Liberty. 'Robbing banks or trains ain't right but it's what outlaws do, we all know that. But murdering a whole bunch of innocent townspeople is truly devil's work. And I reckon even Sloane Wallace will draw the line at that.'

Again, the men murmured in agreement.

'It's settled then,' Mayor Justin said quickly. 'All in favor of setting the Wallace boys free raise your hands.'

Every man present raised his hand.

'Reckon you got your answer,' the mayor told Liberty. 'Now, do your duty and set them free.'

''Fraid I can't do that, Bob.'

'It ain't up to you, dammit! As mayor of Clearwater, I'm giving you a direct order. Turn those men loose at once!'

'You're forgetting something,' Liberty said. 'I'm not your sheriff. You didn't elect me. I'm a Federal officer and I take orders from Marshal Thompson, not you.'

'Then give us the keys and we'll do it for you,' put in Luke Logan. 'We ain't particular how it gets done — not when it comes to saving our necks!'

'You want to save your necks,' Liberty said. 'That's fine with me. Go on home, lock all the doors and windows and pray that the Wallace gang won't come after you. Me, I'll be in Sheriff Hagen's office, with the door barred and the windows shuttered, holding a shotgun aimed at Caleb and Josh Wallace. And if Sloane or Lee or Virge or any of the outlaws tries to break in, they better bring coffins because all they'll find is corpses.' Before anyone could argue with her, she stormed out of the town hall.

Outside, though, as she crossed the dusk-shrouded street and headed for the sheriff's office, she didn't feel as confident as she'd pretended. The Wallace gang was known for their cruelty and vicious reprisals, and Sloane, even without his mother's influence, seemed to find joy in torturing and killing anyone who stood in his way.

* * *

Now, as sundown darkened into evening, lengthening the shadows on Front Street, Liberty sat on an old hardback chair outside the sheriff's office. Her feet were propped up on the post supporting the awning that covered the boardwalk, a shotgun rested across her knees, and her eyes were squinted as she watched the eastern outskirts of Clearwater — knowing this was probably the direction from which the Wallace gang would come.

A noise to her left made her quickly turn and look.

'You again,' she said as Trouble limped out of the darkness. 'Don't worry,' she added as the big white dog paused and eyed her suspiciously, 'I'm not going to bother you. You want to walk around limping that's your business. I've got enough troubles of my own without taking on yours.'

As she spoke the dog came closer and now she saw that it was limping far worse than before. She also noticed its left front paw was caked with blood and every few steps the dog lifted it as if in great pain.

Compassion stirred inside her. Taking a chance of getting bitten, she set the shotgun against the wall, leaned forward so that the front legs of the chair touched down on the boardwalk, and stretched out her hand toward the dog.

Instantly its lips wrinkled back, baring its fangs, and it growled.

Every instinct told her to pull her hand back. Instead, she kept it held out, saying gently: 'Easy, boy . . . easy. Can't you see I'm trying to help you?'

Trouble stopped growling and baring its teeth, and stared at Liberty with its liquid brown eyes.

'You don't let me look at that paw,' she warned, 'it'll end up infected — if it isn't already — and then your days are numbered, Mr. Dog.'

Trouble didn't respond.

'So what's it going to be, fella — you going to be stubborn and end up at Boot Hill or you going to let me look at your paw?'

The dog stared at her for a long moment. Then it flopped down in front of her and rested its massive white head atop its paws.

'Here goes nothing,' Liberty muttered. Rising, she kneeled in front of the dog and carefully inched her hand toward its injured paw. 'Lift your head,' she told it. 'Better yet, lie on your side . . . ' She gently pushed the Great Pyrenees onto its side. It made no attempt to resist; nor to growl or flinch when Liberty reached for its left front paw.

'Okay, now we're getting somewhere . . . ' She lifted the injured paw and examined the blood-caked pad.

'My God,' she murmured as she saw the jagged piece of glass buried in the pad. 'That's really nasty. How the heck did you manage to walk at all?'

Trouble merely stared at her, for the first time in its life putting its trust in a human being.

'This is going to hurt,' Liberty warned. 'But it's the only way you're going to get better.' She grasped the paw with one hand and the piece of the glass between the thumb and finger of the other — and pulled.

Trouble flinched but didn't utter a sound.

Liberty pulled on the glass shard again — and this time it came out of the pad. Blood oozed from the wound. Rising, Liberty held her hand up to the dog, told it to stay and hurried into the office.

Trouble turned its injured paw over and gently licked the blood away.

Moments later Liberty returned beside the dog holding a half-empty bottle of whiskey.

'This will smart some,' she said, uncorking the bottle, 'but it'll stop any infection.' She poured whiskey over the still-bleeding paw. The dog grunted in pain but didn't try to pull its paw out of from Liberty's hand. 'You really should let me bandage that,' she said, corking the bottle, 'but that's probably asking too much. Besides, you'd probably only chew it off anyway.'

Rising, she watched as the giant white dog scrambled up and stood there in front of her, gingerly testing its weight on the injured paw.

'Feel better?'

Trouble looked at her, brown eyes full of gratitude.

Liberty reached out her hand to fondle its huge furry head.

The dog moved faster than she'd expected and grabbed her hand between its jaws.

Caught off-guard, Liberty felt its teeth clamp over her hand and tensed, expecting to be bitten.

Instead, Trouble held her hand firmly

between its jaws but not hard enough to break the skin. Then it shook its head, her hand still gently clamped between its teeth, as if thanking her. Finally, it let her hand go.

'I'll be damned,' Liberty said softly. 'You sure had me worried there for a mo — ' she broke off as she heard a horse galloping into town from the west.

The dog heard it too. Instantly it bared its fangs and snarled in the direction of the approaching rider.

'Easy,' Liberty said. 'It's only Vi'.'

But Trouble was already limping off.

Liberty watched as the dog disappeared down a nearby alley then turned her attention to Violet. He reined up, his lathered horse coming to a slithering halt in front of Liberty. He then stepped down from the saddle and tossed the reins over the hitch-rail.

'Any sign of them yet?' he asked, taking his rifle from its scabbard and joining her.

'Nope.' She walked to the edge of the

boardwalk, shotgun cradled in one arm, squinting into the gloom. 'Did you get Clem settled with the Neilsons?'

Violet nodded. 'Nice folks. Clem took to them right off.'

'Bet they didn't even question why you were leaving her there with them, did they?'

'Nope. I just mentioned your name and they took her in like she was one of their own.' He poked his head inside the empty office, then turned and grinned at her. 'Looks like you've been real successful as a recruiter.'

She took his needling good-naturedly. 'I'm used to it, Vi'. Men have been treating me like poison ivy since as far back as I can remember.'

Violet chuckled and chambered a shell into his Winchester. 'Just shows you how near-sighted they are. Now me,' he said, admiring her, 'I got twenty-twenty vision and I like what I see.'

Liberty smiled, pleased by the compliment. She liked what she saw too, and curious to see how serious he was, said: 'Marshal Macahan used to say it's easy to flatter a girl when there's a storm coming.'

'Ezra's right,' Violet said, settling comfortably in her chair. 'But, then, I've lived most of my life in a storm. And if there's one thing I've learned, it's that the safest place to be is in the eye of that storm.' He looked off up the street to the east, visualizing the Wallace gang riding in. 'So what's coming my way, be it heaven or hell on horseback, I always face it head-on and give as good or better than I get.'

'Now you sound like my father,' Liberty said. 'For as long as I've known him, whether it was as a drifter watering his horse at the Mercer ranch or as my dad fighting alongside me in Mexico, it never mattered what life threw at him. Good or bad, he always accepted it as a challenge — and still does — never whining or gloating no matter the outcome.'

'Shades of Ezra Macahan,' Violet

said. 'They're two of a kind that pair, mirror images you might say — a rare breed that's vanishing faster than the west itself.'

Liberty shrugged as if not altogether agreeing, and looked admiringly at Violet. 'Don't sell yourself short, detective. Times might be changing, and progress might not suit everyone, but there'll always be good men to tame any frontier. Good women, too.' Nodding at the office, she added: 'There's fresh coffee inside. Be happy to fix you a cup while I'm pouring one for myself.'

'I'd like that,' Violet said.

'Black?'

'With enough sugar so the spoon can stand up.'

After Liberty had gone inside, Violet tilted the chair back so that he could lean against the wall and began whistling tunelessly to himself. He liked Liberty, more than he cared to admit, and he hoped that in the next few hours both of them were going to live long

154

enough for him to pursue the feelings she had aroused in him.

Somewhere off in the distance a coyote howled mournfully.

It was definitely going to be a long night, Violet thought as he brushed away the insects whining about his head. But then, he'd never expected it to be anything else.

19

A little later, when the two of them were sitting in the office, drinking coffee on opposite sides of Sheriff Hagen's desk, there was a faint thud outside the door.

Alarmed, they drew their six-guns. Liberty quickly blew out the hurricane lamp on the desk, throwing the room into darkness save for the pale moonlight shining in through the window.

Already on his feet, Violet signaled for Liberty to cover him. She nodded, ready to shoot if need be, while he inched open the door.

No one was there. Giving her a puzzled look, Violet poked his head out and looked up and down the street. Empty. He turned and shook his head at her to indicate that he'd seen nothing threatening.

It was then Liberty noticed the gray

furry lump lying on the boardwalk in front of Violet's feet. She moved close, hunkered down and picked it up.

'What the hell . . . ?' began Violet.

Liberty chuckled, 'Just a friend of mine repaying a debt,' and tossed the dead rabbit on the table. 'It'll make a fine stew.'

Relieved, Violet holstered his Colt, locked the door and studied the furry corpse. 'Kind of an odd way to repay a debt.'

'He's kind of an odd friend,' Liberty said.

'He?' Violet questioned.

'Uh-huh.'

'Anyone I know?'

'Most likely.'

'A suitor?'

'Maybe. I'm not sure yet.'

'You never told me you had a suitor.'

'Didn't know I had until just now.'

'Does he live here — in town?'

'Could say that.'

Liberty deliberately made it sound mysterious and Violet took the bait.

'Where?'

'Not sure exactly.'

'He's a suitor and you don't know where he lives?'

'Said he *may* be a suitor.'

Violet grunted. 'What else do you know about him?'

'Well . . . he's something of a loner.'

'That ain't a good sign.'

'Hasn't the best disposition either.'

'That's two strikes against him.'

'But he can be a real charmer, too.'

'Charmers can't be trusted. I hate charmers.'

'You wouldn't hate him. Nobody hates him. In fact he's looked on very favorably around town.'

'How long you been seeing him?'

'Not long.'

Violet scowled. 'Should I be jealous?'

'Hard to say,' Liberty said, straight-faced. 'I mean he's younger than you. And far more cuddly. Some folks might think he's better looking, too.'

'Good looks are overrated,' Violet said dismissively.

'And he has these beautiful, big, soulful brown eyes.'

'Most women I know prefer steely blue or gray, like mine.'

Liberty almost laughed.

'Anything else I should know about him?' Violet demanded.

'Well, as you can see,' she said, indicating the dead rabbit, 'he repays his debts, which shows he has integrity.'

Stumped, Violet said grudgingly: 'Reckon I can't argue with integrity.'

'It's a desirable trait and one mighty hard to come-by,' Liberty agreed. Deciding that she'd teased him long enough, she was about to confess that his rival was a dog, when she heard the sound of a horse galloping along the street toward them.

Violet heard it too. Looking out the window, he held up one finger to indicate only one rider.

Drawing her Colt, Liberty joined Violet and peered through the glass.

'Who is it, can you see?'

'Not yet, but — '

'What?' she said as he paused.

Violet said only: 'Dammit to hell!'

'What's wrong?'

Expelling his exasperation in an angry sigh, he holstered his gun and opened the door.

Liberty quickly peered over his shoulder and recognized the rider reining up outside.

'Mother Mary,' she breathed. 'I don't believe it!' Pushing past Violet, she stormed outside.

Violet remained in the doorway, watching as the rider jumped off the lathered, unsaddled horse and joined Liberty on the boardwalk.

'You better have one God Almighty good reason for being here,' Liberty said angrily.

'I do,' Clem said — and fainted into Liberty's arms.

'Oh-dear-God,' Liberty exclaimed as she saw the blood on Clem's shirt-sleeve. 'She's been shot!'

Violet quickly gathered Clem up in his arms and carried her into the office.

There, he waited until Liberty had lit the lamp and cleared everything off the desk before gently setting Clem down. He then rolled back her sleeve and examined the wound.

'It's not bad,' he said, relieved. 'See, just a nick.'

'Who'd shoot a child?' Liberty said.

Violet didn't answer. Instead he ransacked the desk drawers until he found a near-empty bottle of whiskey. Uncorking it, he told Liberty to hold Clem still. When she did, he poured whiskey over the wound, sterilizing it, then tilted the bottle against Clem's lips and forced a few drops down her throat.

She came around, choking and gagging, eyes popping open, looking around trying to establish where she was. On seeing Liberty and Violet, she sat up, and almost incoherently began to babble. 'They're coming! — All of 'em! — Be here soon! — Tried to stop me but I out-foxed 'em — jumped on a horse and got away 'fore they could catch me an' so they shot me as I rode away and — '

'Whoa, whoa,' Violet said, cutting her off. 'Calm down, missy.'

'Who's coming,' Liberty asked. ' — your brothers?'

'Uh-huh. Sloane an' Virge an' Lee an' a bunch of — '

'How far are they behind you?'

'I dunno. But as I was riding away I could hear Sloane yelling for everyone to mount up and — '

'Who shot you?'

'Don't know that neither. Could've been Lee or Virge or — '

'Surely your own brothers wouldn't shoot you?' Liberty said.

'You don't know my brothers.'

'What about the Neilsons?' Violet interrupted. 'Did you see if — ?'

'They're dead,' Clem said. 'Sloane gunned 'em down when he found out they was hiding me!'

'Judas,' Violet breathed.

'What's worse, they was unarmed and he never even give 'em a chance.'

Liberty paled and angrily clenched her teeth. 'What about their sons — Leif and Erik? Sloane kill them, too?'

Clem shrugged. 'I ain't sure. Mr. Neilson said they rode off 'fore sunup to round up some strays and — and they hadn't come back by the time my brothers showed . . . so . . . but if they heard the shooting . . . maybe they came back . . . or . . . I don't know,' she said, shrugging again. 'I was too busy riding here to tell you.'

Liberty fondly put her arm around Clem. 'Thank you. That was brave of you . . . '

'Truly brave,' said Violet. 'And we appreciate it.'

'Then you ain't sore at me?'

''Course not,' Liberty said. 'You risked your life for us and we're very grateful. Right, Vi'?'

He nodded and gently kissed Clem on the forehead. 'More than you'll ever know, missy. Now, you sit still, right there, while I find some bandages and take care of that wound.'

20

The night wore on without any sign of the outlaws. Liberty and Violet took turns sleeping, relieving each other every couple of hours, while Clem slept on a bunk that Violet had dragged from an empty cell and put in the corner of the office.

Daylight came. 'Maybe we guessed wrong,' Violet said, yawning, when Liberty brought him a mug of coffee. 'Maybe Sloane figured the odds were against them and decided that trying to break out his brothers wasn't worth possibly getting killed.'

Liberty went on sipping her coffee in silence.

'You're right,' Violet agreed. 'I don't believe it for a second, either.'

Liberty finished her coffee, went to the stove and refilled her cup, then came and stood sipping from it at the window beside Violet. 'My guess is they'll hit us while we're taking Josh and Caleb to the station.'

Violet spoke to her reflection in the window. 'It's how I'd do it.'

'What do you think about getting there early — to the station-house, I mean — before Sloane and his men have a chance to hole up there and ambush us?'

'You're reading my mind, deputy. But if it's going to work, we need to move the prisoners while it's still dark.' He looked up at the faint lemony streaks that were starting to lighten the overcast sky. 'Means we got to do it pretty soon.'

'How about now?' Liberty said. Gulping the last of her coffee, she took a Winchester from the gun-rack and a box of cartridges from the drawer below; then grabbing the keys off the hook unlocked the door leading to the cells. 'Keep watching the street while I bring them out,' she told Violet. 'Oh, and wake Clem up. We're going to have to take her along. It's not what I wanted, but for the moment it's the safest bet.'

'How 'bout one suggestion?'

'I'm listening.'

'We only take Caleb and Josh with us on this trip.'

'What about the other two — they're all part of the Wallace gang.'

'I know. But two's easier to handle if shooting starts. 'Sides, you can always bring them another time or have the sheriff bring 'em to Guthrie for you — that's if he turns out to be honest.'

Liberty mulled the idea over, saw the sense in it and nodded.

'Oh, and something else,' added Violet.

'You said one suggestion.'

'I know. But I'm feeling extra smart this morning.'

'I'll be the judge of that,' Liberty said, but she was smiling as she spoke.

'I once had to take a prisoner to the train station — in Buffalo, Wyoming, it was. Town was full of his pals, all hoping to shoot my guts out if they got the chance.'

'So?'

'I rigged a shotgun so that the barrel was tied pointing at his head, while the stock was fastened to my wrist. I kept my finger on the trigger the whole time we walked, so that even if someone shot me in the back, I would've still blown his skull off as I fell.'

Liberty chuckled. 'I do so admire ingenuity, Mr. Flowers.'

'Enough to give me a badge?' he deadpanned.

'Aww, hell . . . ' She opened the desk drawer, rummaged through its contents and pulled out something shiny. 'Here,' she tossed a Deputy Sheriff's star to Violet. 'This'll have to do for now.'

Ten minutes later the five of them left the sheriff's office. The sun was just coming up over the hills to the east, its rays striping the rooftops but the yellow orb not yet high enough to cause shadows on Front Street.

Violet, with a shotgun fastened to

each forearm, the barrels tied against the back of the outlaws' necks, a finger on each trigger, walked ahead of Liberty and Clem. Both of them carried rifles, Clem making sure no one appeared on their right, Liberty doing the same on their left.

'Watch the rooftops,' she warned as they approached the cross-street separating them from the little yellow-and-brown station-house. 'Not just the alleys and doorways.'

'I am, I am,' Clem said.

They continued on up the shadowy, empty, silent street.

'You just wasting your time, deputy,' Caleb told Liberty. 'Even if my brothers don't bust us loose here, they'll do it on the train or at the other end, in Guthrie.'

'I'm counting on it,' Liberty said sweetly. 'It'll give me a legal reason to shoot you both.'

'And if she can't find one,' Violet added, 'I will — legal or not.'

They reached the cross street. Ahead,

beyond the tracks fronting the station-house, the barren flatlands stretched farther than one could see in the lavender dawn light. A wind moaned in off the wasteland, blowing warm dust in their faces.

'See any horses tied up anywhere?' Violet said to Liberty.

'Uh-uh. Why, you think they're already there, holed up inside?'

'Possible.'

'Maybe I should go ahead and look?'

'Nah. Splitting your force in half's never a good idea — ask Custer.'

'That's a cheerful thought.'

'Never underestimate your enemy.'

'Caution's the way.'

'Know what?' Clem broke in irritably, 'I'd sure 'preciate it if you two would quit 'whistling 'round tombstones.' It's hell on my nerves.'

Liberty and Violet chuckled softly and fell silent.

They crossed the intersection and cautiously approached the station-house. No lights showed inside. The

169

wind came again, stronger this time, causing a loose board somewhere to bang aimlessly against the woodwork. Violet stopped, as did Liberty and Clem behind him, and whispered to the Wallace brothers:

'Reckon if anyone's inside, they've already seen these shotguns I got rigged against your necks. But in case they haven't, I suggest you holler out and explain the situation to your brothers so I don't have pull these triggers.'

'I ain't saying nothing,' Josh said. 'Not one goddamn word.'

'Me, neither,' said Caleb.

Violet shrugged. 'Suit yourselves. It's your funeral. Me, I'm just trying to clear my conscience 'case I have to spatter your brains all over the street.'

Caleb had second thoughts. 'Hey!' he yelled. 'You in the station-house. Don't shoot. They got shotguns tied to us. We're dead for sure if'n you do.'

No answer.

The wind died and the monotonous bang-banging stopped.

A horse whinnied in the distance, but the sound came from the direction of the livery stable.

'That's Regret,' Liberty said. 'Must've heard my voice.'

They moved closer, within a few steps of the station-house now. Still no sound could be heard inside.

'Get behind me,' Liberty told Clem.

'Why? I ain't scared.'

'Then you're the only one here who isn't,' Violet said. 'Now do as Liberty says. Get behind her.'

Grudgingly, Clem obeyed.

'Go ahead,' Violet said as Josh and Caleb paused. 'Keep moving.'

The Wallace brothers grudgingly moved forward, one slow step-at-a-time, until they reached the station-house. There, Violet looked back at Liberty, who nodded for him to go ahead. She then motioned that she'd be right behind him. He nodded to show he understood and prodded the prisoners with the shotguns, forcing them to step up onto the low wooden platform

171

on which the station-house was built. He cautiously followed them and a step behind him, came Liberty and Clem.

They trod lightly, trying to lessen the noise of their footsteps on the sun-bleached planking. The wind sprang up again. It came moaning in off the wasteland stretched out in front of them, causing the same loose board to start bang-banging again, at the same time forcing them to squint in order to keep the dust out of their eyes.

They reached the waiting-room door. It was closed. There was no light on inside. Telling Violet to wait, Liberty peered in the window. But it was too dark inside for her to see anything more than the shadowy outlines of the two waiting benches and the office ticket window facing them.

'Looks empty to me,' she told Violet. She tried the door but it was locked. 'Did you hear that?' she whispered.

'Hear what?'

'That noise? When I tried the door? Sounded like a . . . low rumbling noise.'

'Just the wind,' Violet said. 'Don't go gettin' spooky on me.'

'What d'you expect?' she said sarcastically. 'I'm only a poor helpless woman.'

'Helpless my ass,' he said. Then indicating the door: 'Kick it in. We're sitting ducks out here.'

'Wait,' Clem said, pointing. 'Window ain't locked.'

Liberty peered closer, saw that the slide-lock was indeed open, wedged her fingers under the top of the lower frame and pushed upward. 'Good call,' she told Clem as the window slid up. 'Now climb in and unlock the door for us. Hurry.'

Clem obeyed. But as she swung her legs over the window sill and stepped into the waiting room, there was a sudden angry snarl and something huge leaped out of the darkness, knocking Clem down. She screamed, but didn't move as whatever knocked her down stood over her, growling.

Liberty quickly leaned in the window,

ready to shoot Clem's attacker.

'Holy mother,' she exclaimed. Then to Violet behind her: 'Let me handle this.' Holstering her gun, she spoke calmly to Clem: 'Don't move, girl, till I tell you . . . '

Clem gave a stifled whimper and fell quiet.

Liberty looked at the great white dog straddling Clem and said gently but firmly: 'It's okay, fella. No one's going to hurt you . . . Let her up, okay? Go on . . . do as I say . . . Get back . . . now . . . Hear me? Go on, boy . . . let her up.'

Trouble looked up at Liberty, fangs bared, but no longer growling.

'Go on,' Liberty urged softly. 'Do as I say. Get back . . . '

Trouble stopped baring its teeth and seemed to relax. Slowly it stepped away from Clem and stood there in the semi-darkness, motionless, eyes fixed on Liberty as she climbed in through the window.

'It's all right,' Liberty assured Clem.

'You can get up now.'

'W-What about him?'

'He won't hurt you. Promise.' She helped Clem up and felt her shaking.

'Is she okay?' Violet said, looking in through the open window.

'Sure,' Liberty replied. 'Just scared her a bit is all.'

'Thought he was gonna k-kill me,' Clem said, eyeing the dog. 'Why'd he attack me anyways?'

Before Liberty could answer, Trouble padded to the far wall, nudged aside a loose board with its nose and squeezed out into the night.

'Guess we now know where he sleeps,' Liberty said. 'Climbing in like that, Clem, you must have startled him.'

'I only done like you told me.'

'I'm not blaming you. I'm just — '

Violet, weary of their chatter, said: 'I hate to break up the party, ladies, but will one of you open the damn door, so I can get these boys in off the street?'

'Sorry . . . ' Clem hurried to the

door, opened it, then stood back so Violet and the Wallace brothers could enter. They glared at Clem as they passed her.

'Me'n Caleb ain't forgetting what you done,' Josh hissed at her.

'Us being your own kin and all,' Caleb said.

'Should've thought of that 'fore you let Sloane kill Pa,' Clem said.

'What was we supposed to do?' Caleb whined. 'It's what Ma wanted and you know Ma — she always gets what she wants.'

'Could've at least warned him,' Clem said bitterly. 'Or tried to hide him till he sobered up. 'Least then he would've had a chance to defend hisself.'

'All right, that's enough,' Liberty said. 'You can settle your family quarrels later.' Then to Violet: 'Untie those shotguns. We've got a long wait ahead of us. Train isn't due for another two hours or so.'

'Good idea . . . ' He prodded the brothers over to the window, adding:

176

'Keep a sharp eye on them. Either one so much as blinks while I'm working on these knots, shoot him.'

'Be my pleasure,' Liberty said. Then to Clem: 'Help Mr. Flowers. But don't get between me and your brothers. Clear?'

Clem nodded. She waited until Liberty covered her brothers with the rifle and then helped Violet unknot the cords holding the shotguns to his forearms. Once they were untied, he told her to step back. When she did, he loosened the cords holding the shotguns against the necks of the two prisoners.

It took a few minutes but finally it was done. Violet stepped back, a shotgun in each hand, and told the brothers to sit on one of the benches. They obeyed and sat there glaring at Clem in surly silence . . .

21

By now the sun was fully up. Through the window they could see its light reflecting off the tracks and, beyond the intersection, Front Street leading back into town. It was still empty but here and there lights were being turned on in the various buildings, indicating the town was slowly coming to life.

'What time do you reckon the station-master will get here?' Violet asked Liberty.

'Seven o'clock, sharp.'

'Why so early? Train isn't due till eight-fifteen.'

'True. But Mr. McCullen, he's a meticulous bird who insists on order in his life. Every morning before any passengers arrive, he makes sure the benches are dusted, the brass is shined, floor's swept, spittoons empty, no fingerprints on the windows . . . and there's money in the cash-drawer for folks who don't have the correct change for their ticket.'

'Sounds like someone I couldn't live with.'

'His wife felt the same way. Poor woman moved out shortly after they got hitched and he's been alone ever since.'

'Wonder if he knows that dog sleeps here at night?' Clem said.

'I'd bet my life he doesn't,' Liberty said. 'I'd also bet he doesn't know that board's loose, either — or he'd nail it shut and keep Trouble out of here.'

'I never liked him,' Clem said. 'Neither did Pa.'

'You aren't alone. His fussiness riles a lot of folks.'

Clem smirked. 'Can't wait to see his face when he finds us all in here ahead of him. He's sure to throw ten fits.'

'Once I explain why we're here,' Liberty said, 'he'll calm down. He won't have any choice.'

'Won't matter none either way,' Caleb sneered. 'You won't be alive to tell him. None of you will.'

'Still think your brothers are coming for you?' Liberty said.

'Can count on it. Same as you can count on gettin' the thrashing of your life,' he said to Clem. ' — even if I have to give it to you myself.'

'Can add me to that list,' growled Josh. 'Just something to look forward to, little sister.'

'To hell with you,' Clem said defiantly.

Violet looked at Liberty and Clem. 'Why don't you two ladies go get some fresh air for a few minutes? That way I can have a nice friendly chat with these two weasels.'

'Forget it,' Liberty said. ''Case you've forgotten, Deputy Flowers, you're wearing a badge now.'

'Can always take it off.'

'Won't change anything. Badge or no badge, there'll be no vigilante justice around here — not so long as I'm in charge.'

Violet sighed and winked at Clem.

'Every job has its drawbacks.'

She started to grin then stopped as she spotted movement out in the street. 'Look,' she pointed, 'someone's coming!'

They moved to the window and saw a lone rider trotting toward them.

'Well, I'll be damned,' Liberty murmured as she recognized the rider. 'Sheriff Hagen.'

'Reckon we misjudged him,' Violet said. 'Either that or he didn't feel as poorly as he pretended.'

'How'd he know we was here?' Clem asked.

'Put two-and-two together, most likely,' Liberty said. 'Since we weren't in his office and he knows I'm taking your brothers to Guthrie this morning, where else would we be.'

'Don't forget those two snakes you left in jail,' reminded Violet, 'could be they told him.' As he spoke he noticed both Josh and Caleb were smirking. It raised the hair on his neck and grabbing one of the shotguns, he thumbed the triggers back, saying to Liberty: 'Watch 'em for me.'

'Where you going?' she demanded.

'Have a word with Sheriff Hagen.' He pushed past her, opened the door and stepped outside before she could stop him.

'Damn,' she said crossly.

'Don't be sore at him,' Clem said. 'He's just trying to protect us. I mean, you did make him your deputy.'

'Yes, but deputies are supposed to be taking orders, not giving them.' Grumbling, Liberty trained her rifle on the two Wallace brothers, at the same time trying to keep an eye on the window so she could see what Sheriff Hagen was doing.

'That's close enough,' she heard Violet call out.

Outside, Sheriff Hagen reined up on the other side of the cross-street.

'Keep your hands where I can see 'em,' Violet ordered. Then as the sheriff rested both hands atop the saddle-horn: 'What do you want?'

'Deputy Mercer — she inside?'

'Yep.'

'I need to talk to her.'

'Talk to me,' Violet said. 'If I think it's important enough, I'll pass it along.'

'You?' Sheriff Hagen sputtered. 'Who the hell are you to question — ?'

'It's all right. Let him talk, Vi'. I can hear him plain enough,' Liberty shouted from in the station-house. 'Go ahead, Will. What's on your mind?'

'The Wallace gang is headed this way,' he said. 'They stopped by my place 'bout an hour ago — told me to tell you that if you let their brothers go, they'll ride on peaceably.'

'And if I don't?'

'They'll turn Clearwater into a bloodbath.'

'Sorry. No deal.'

'For God's sake, Liberty — '

Violet stopped him. 'You heard her, you mealy-mouthed weasel. Now go back and tell your gutless pals that if they come busting in here, they'll never see their brothers alive again. 'Cause

183

win, lose or draw I'll personally put a bullet in their brains before I'll let them walk free.'

'You'll live to regret those words,' Sheriff Hagen said.

'I doubt it,' Violet said. He tapped his breast pocket. 'I got papers on me, legal papers signed by the President himself, giving me the authority to arrest every member of the Wallace gang — arrest 'em and bring them in, *dead or alive,* all in the name of justice.'

'Justice ain't got nothing to do with this,' the sheriff said angrily. 'This is all about saving folks' lives. Innocent folks. Men, women and young'uns who settled here to make a life for themselves.'

'Men, women and young'uns who agreed to obey the law,' Liberty said. 'A law you swore to uphold, in case it's slipped your memory, Will.'

'I know what I swore to uphold,' he said. 'But I also know that there comes a time when common sense outweighs even the law — and this is one of them times. Dammit, Liberty, surely you can see that, can't you?'

She took a deep breath, feeling like she had the survival of Clearwater resting on her shoulders, and then expelled all her frustration in a long sigh.

'You got my answer, Will. Do what you want with it. But remember this: no matter how many threats I get, when that train pulls in, I'll be boarding it with my two prisoners.'

'Same goes for me,' Violet said. 'Only difference is I don't give a hoot if they're alive or dead!'

Sheriff Hagen scowled in disgust. 'You're damn fools,' he said, 'both of you — fools who won't live to see tomorrow!' Wheeling his horse around, he rode off in the direction he'd come . . .

22

As Liberty predicted, at exactly seven o'clock the station-master, Rupert McCullen, put his key in the lock and started to unlock the door — then stopped as he realized it was already unlocked. Even more of a surprise, the door was suddenly opened from the inside and facing him stood Deputy U.S. Marshal Liberty Mercer.

He jumped back with a startled gasp and stared at her as if she were an apparition.

'Quick,' she said, grabbing his spindly arm, 'get inside!'

He resisted, but she jerked him toward her and he stumbled into the waiting-room. There, on seeing Violet seated on a bench, shotgun across his knees, opposite the Wallace brothers, he shrank back, 'Oh, dear,' and turned to run.

'Hold it!' Liberty blocked his path to the door. 'Sorry to scare you, Mr. McCullen, but I had no choice but to bring them here. Not if I wanted to get these two men on the train without a lot of shooting.'

The word 'shooting' seemed to frighten him even more.

'B-But you can't use firearms,' he stammered. 'There'll be people here — other passengers. They might be killed if — '

Violet stopped him. Pulling out a wallet displaying his railroad detective credentials, he held it up to the gaunt, balding station-master and explained who he was. 'What's more,' he went on, 'I'll take full responsibility for anything that happens. Okay?'

Before the bewildered McCullen could more than nod, Clem chimed in: 'Did you know you got a big white dog sleeps here at night?'

'A w-what?' said McCullen.

'Not now, sweetheart,' Liberty said, trying to hush Clem.

But it was too late. McCullen's owlish gray eyes widened behind his metal-frame spectacles. 'Dog?' he said aghast. 'What dog? What're you talking about?'

'That big white dog — you know, the one that's always wandering 'round town — he sneaks in through that loose board there and sleeps here at night.'

'Oh, dear God,' said McCullen. 'There must be fleas everywhere — '

'Never mind the damn' fleas,' Liberty said. 'or the dog — '

'But I hate dogs — '

' — just concentrate on what I'm telling you.' She grasped the lapels of his black suit and forced him to look at her. 'You listening to me?'

'Y-Yes.'

'Okay then. This is what I want you to do. I want you to get on the wire and contact Oklahoma City — find out if the train's going to be on time.'

'Why shouldn't it be on time?' he said, alarmed. 'Has there been a collision or a robbery somewhere?'

'Not that I know of.'

'Then — ?'

'Goddammit,' Violet broke in, 'don't stand there babbling, you old goat. You heard Deputy Mercer. Do as she says. Now — or I'll have you fired!'

McCullen came alive, 'Y-Yessir! Right away, sir!' and hurried into his office. They heard him sit down and start tap-tapping on the telegraph machine. Almost immediately, he received a reply. And when he rejoined them a few minutes later, he assured them that the train was on time. 'Should be here in' — he took out his big Hamilton fob watch and checked the time — 'fifty-eight minutes.'

Clem stopped looking out the window and turned to Liberty. 'Wagon's coming up the street . . . and some folks are opening their stores.'

Liberty and Violet quickly joined her. Outside, approaching from the far end of town was a freight-wagon, drawn by a team of mules. It ground to a halt in front of Greenwood Mercantile.

'It's okay,' Liberty said, referring to the driver, a burly man in coveralls who jumped down and plodded to the rear of the big wagon. 'That's Hank Catlin — old man Greenwood's son-in-law. He's been handling the store's freight for years.'

'Let's hope nobody's hiding in that wagon,' Violet said.

'It's a chance I'll have to take,' Liberty said.

'Why? Where you going?'

'To clear everyone off the street.'

'I'll go with you.'

'No. You stay here and drag one of those benches over in front of the window. It'll give us protection once the shooting starts.'

'What about him?' Violet said, nodding at the station-master.

'Get in your office and lock the door,' she told McCullen. 'Don't come out, no matter what, until I tell you. And you, young lady,' she said to Clem, 'you do exactly what Mr. Flowers tells you. Got that?'

'Yes'm.'

'Make it quick,' Violet said as he opened the door for Liberty. 'You don't want to be caught out in the street should our 'friends' arrive.'

Liberty smiled wryly. 'Worried about me — *deputy?*'

'Damn right I am.' With dramatic exaggeration he polished his deputy badge with his sleeve. 'If you get shot, it'll be a blemish on my spotless record.'

Liberty chuckled, opened the door and stepped outside.

Violet stood in the doorway, ready to shoot anyone threatening; then, when Liberty reached Front Street and told the storekeepers to get in their stores and stay there, he closed the door and asked Clem to give him a hand.

Together, they dragged one of the benches over in front of the window and turned it on its side. He then told her to hunker down behind it and keep her eyes peeled.

'Don't worry,' she said. 'Soon as I see

my brothers ridin' in, I'll holler out.'

'They may not ride in, missy. Could be they'll leave their horses outside town and sneak in. You know. Use the buildings as cover until they're close enough to get a bead on us.'

'Either way I'll be ready for them,' she vowed. 'You just be sure not to turn your back on Josh or Caleb. You do and those slab-heads will find a way to shoot you in the back.'

Violet looked at the two outlaws. 'Been thinking about that. And the way I figure it, the only way I can trust 'em is if they're asleep.'

'Fat chance of that,' growled Josh.

'Oh, I don't know . . . ' Violet stepped close, grabbed both men by their hair and jerked them forward so that they fell sprawling on the floor. 'You'd be surprised how easy it is to fall asleep.' He swung his shotgun, clubbing the outlaws on the back of the head. They slumped over, unconscious. 'See,' he grinned. 'That wasn't so difficult, was it?'

Clem giggled. 'They gonna be awful riled when they wake up, Mr. Flowers.'

'I know. That's why I'm going to hog-tie 'em before they do.' Removing his belt, he dragged the legs of both brothers alongside each other and tied them together. 'That ought to do it,' he said.

Clem nodded, turned back to the window, saying: 'I wish that darn train would hurry up and get here. Then we wouldn't need to get in no shootout with Sloane and the others.'

'It's a nice thought, missy. But not one I'd count on — not if what Sheriff Hagan said is true.' There was a scraping noise behind them. Both whirled around, ready to shoot; then relaxed as they saw the loose board pushed aside by Trouble's nose, allowing the big white dog to squeeze through. Once inside it stopped and eyed them suspiciously.

'Look, he's hurt his paw,' Clem pointed. Before Violet could stop her, she kneeled in front of Trouble and reached for his blood-stained front paw.

'Careful,' warned Violet. 'He might bite if — ' He didn't bother to finish as the dog allowed Clem to examine his injured foot.

'He's been cut . . . Oh, you poor thing . . . Look,' she said, holding the paw up to Violet. 'There's blood caked all around the pad.'

'When we've got time, we'll wash it clean, missy. Meanwhile, at least the wound's stopped bleeding and seems to be healing.' He went to pat the dog's massive furry head then quickly jerked his hand back as Trouble bared his fangs in a silent snarl. 'Okay, okay . . . relax, fella . . . I'm just trying to help. Obviously he prefers you to me,' he said to Clem.

'Most likely 'cause I'm a girl, like Marshal Liberty.'

'Could be. But for now, why don't you have him lie down under the other bench? That way, he won't be in our way if it comes to shooting.'

Clem nodded and gently grasped the

thick, mane-like ruff around the dog's neck. 'C'mon, boy,' she said, leading it to the bench. 'C'mon . . . over here . . . that's it . . . Now, lie down. It can't hurt too much,' she said as Trouble flopped down under the bench. 'He's barely limping.'

Violet nodded, turned back to the window and saw that Liberty was returning. Opening the door, he stood there on the planking, watching both sides of the street as she walked toward him.

'No sign of them yet,' she said as she came up. 'But everyone feels like we do — it's just a matter of time.'

23

But as time passed, and the clock on the waiting-room wall got closer and closer to eight-fifteen, there was still no sign of the outlaws.

'This waiting's making my nerves crawl,' Liberty said.

'Mine too,' Violet said. He joined her in the doorway and they stood there, rifles cocked, watching the empty street.

'What's stopping them? Why the devil don't they make their play and get it over with?'

'Good question.' Violet scratched a match on the overturned bench, lit his hand-rolled and flipped the match out through the door. He then turned to Clem, who sat on the floor beside the big white dog, saying: 'You know your brothers better than we do. Why do you think they haven't hit us?'

Clem shrugged. 'I don't know. They should be here by now. 'Less'n . . . '

'Unless what?' Violet said as she paused.

''Less'n Ma told them not to. But that ain't likely. No way she's gonna let you or Miss Liberty take her precious Caleb to Guthrie, not when she knows he's most likely facing a rope.'

The office door inched open and McCullen's face peered out through the crack. 'Train's almost due,' he told Liberty. 'I need to get out there on the platform in case the conductor's got something important to tell me.'

Liberty looked at the clock, saw it was nine minutes after eight. She sighed wearily and made a tough decision. 'When the train actually pulls in and folks start getting off, if — *if* her brothers haven't showed, you go out and tell the conductor that we're coming aboard with two prisoners. Got that?'

The station-master nodded and nervously wet his lips. 'What if there is shooting, marshal? What am I supposed to do then?'

'Stay in your office. Keep your head down till it's over, one way or another.' Turning to Violet, she said: 'You stick with Clem, here. Make sure she gets on board safely.'

'Consider it done.' He looked at Caleb and Josh. Conscious now, they sat groggily on the floor, each gingerly rubbing his head. 'Want me to put these two back to sleep? That way we can carry them onto the train. Might be less trouble.'

Liberty shrugged as if it didn't matter either way. 'Your call,' she told the outlaws. 'You want to walk peacefully to the train or be carried?'

'Walk,' Josh said quickly.

'Then that's settled.' She paused as she heard a distant train whistle, and then said to Violet: 'Untie that belt and get them on their feet. But keep them here until I signal that it's all clear . . . then bring them out.'

'Will do.'

Liberty stepped outside and gazed off in the direction of the train.

'What about me?' Clem asked Violet.

'Stick close to me and do exactly as I tell you, just like Liberty said.'

Outside, there was another long, drawn-out whistle. The train was close enough now for Liberty to feel the ground shaking faintly underfoot.

Shading her eyes from the early morning sun, she stared off toward the east. At first all she saw was an empty, early-morning horizon. Then gradually she spotted black smoke curling upward in the heat-wavering distance. Squinting, she made out the shape of the train below the smoke.

Slowly, it came ever-closer, its pounding wheels following the shiny steel tracks that had been laid string-straight across the barren wasteland. Liberty could see the sunlight glinting on the polished brass of the engine, the tall top-heavy smokestack belching black smoke and below, the round face-like front with its bulky headlight and cow-catcher jutting out like an iron beard; at the same instant she tingled with excitement and anticipation mixed with fear and immediately recalled Marshal Thompson's words of advice when he'd first offered her the job as Deputy U.S. Marshal.

'Most of the time,' he said fatherly, 'being a marshal or a deputy ain't as exciting or rewarding as it sounds. Mostly, it comes down to long days in the saddle, aching backsides, sleeping on the ground, living off hardtack, beans and sour coffee, with folks always expecting you to do the right thing — even if it costs you your life. But on the other hand it's an honest, decent way to make a livin' . . . and if you're lucky enough to occasionally get it right and bring a killer to justice, then somehow all the grunt-work seems worth it . . . '

Well, she thought as she watched the train approaching, *I sure hope all this turns out to be worth it.*

★ ★ ★

Violet kept his shotgun trained on the Wallace brothers as the train ground to a shuddering, brake-screeching halt alongside the station-house. Through the open door he saw Liberty walking slowly along the narrow platform, rifle held ready, her head swiveling left and right as she checked for any sign of the outlaws.

Only six passengers got off the train. She recognized four of them and the other two didn't look threatening.

Satisfied that all seemed normal, Liberty signaled to the station-master, who stood anxiously waiting at the window, to come ahead. He darted out the door and hurried toward the conductor who stood next to the caboose.

'Make it quick,' she shouted, 'then get back inside, *pronto*!'

He waved to show he'd heard and continued on his way.

Liberty turned to the door where

Violet now stood with his prisoners, awaiting her signal to bring them out. 'There's room in this car,' she said, thumbing at the last passenger car beside her. 'I'll let you know when to come ahead.'

He nodded and keeping his shotgun pressed against Caleb's ribs, said: 'What about Clem?'

Liberty took another look in both directions. 'Send her out now.'

Violet obeyed.

Liberty saw Clem running toward her and pointed at the nearest boarding steps. 'Find a seat, young lady — any seat — and stay put. Got that?'

'Yes'm.' Clem quickly climbed inside.

Liberty and Violet watched as they caught glimpses of her through the windows as she moved along the aisle between passengers and finally took a seat near the rear door. She waved to Liberty to show she was all right and then looked out the window, anxious to see if her brothers showed.

Liberty, tired of waiting for the

station-master to finish talking to the conductor, ordered him to get back inside. McCullen scowled at her, said a few last words to the conductor and hurried back to the station-house.

Liberty gave a careful look around and then waved for Violet to come out. He obeyed, using the shotguns to prod the prisoners ahead of him.

All the passengers seated beside the windows watched, wide-eyed, as the two Wallace brothers, hands still tied behind them, walked to the train.

Liberty accompanied them to the boarding platform of the last car. There, rifle aimed at Caleb and Josh, she slowly backed up the steps into the car, all the time motioning with her head for them to follow her.

They obeyed, Josh first, Caleb behind him, Violet constantly reminding them that he was there by jabbing them in the back with the shotguns.

Finally, they were all inside. Liberty wagged her rifle at four empty seats facing each other. 'Sit,' she told the outlaws. When they obeyed, she and Violet sat opposite them, weapons resting across their lap.

Outside, the conductor signaled to the engineer all was clear, yelled, 'Allaboar-r-rd,' and swung up onto the caboose. The locomotive spun its wheels, steam gushing out, and slowly lurched forward.

As it did, gradually gaining momentum, a furry white blur raced out of the station-house. It ran alongside the train for a short distance, keeping pace with it and finally jumped onto the boarding platform of the last passenger car. There, it flopped down, panting, and rested its massive square head atop its paws.

Trouble had arrived.

24

As the train headed northwest toward Guthrie, Liberty tried to read the expressions of Caleb and Josh, hoping by doing so she'd understand how they felt about their brothers not making any attempt to rescue them. She studied their sullen faces, wondering if they were as surprised as she was, or whether they had never expected to be broken out of jail in the first place. For all she knew, someone connected to the Wallace gang had managed to get word to them that their rescue was planned to happen elsewhere — while they were aboard the train perhaps or if not then, as they were being transferred from the train to the jail in Guthrie.

But hard as she studied them, she was unable to get any sense of how either brother felt or was thinking. Frustrated, she finally turned to Violet, who was seated beside her, and said softly, so only he could hear: 'They don't look too happy, do they?'

Violet, who'd been watching the two brothers for the same reason, shook his head.

'Think they're faking it for our sakes?'

'Dunno. But somehow I doubt it.'

'Me, too.'

'So what do you make of it? You figure that means they truly expected Sloane and the others to rush us at the station, same as we did?'

'That'd be my guess. But that's all it is — a guess.'

'Yeah, but I think it's the right one,' Violet said. He sighed, adding: 'Tell you the truth, this whole damn thing has thrown me for a loop. I mean, like you, I would've bet the bank that they'd hit us before we pulled out.'

'Puts a new spin on what Sheriff Hagen told us,' Liberty said ' — about the Wallace gang being on his heels, so to speak.'

'It surely does.' Violet frowned, perplexed. 'I just wish I could figure out what their actual plan is.'

'Why they didn't jump us, you mean?'

He nodded. 'There must be a reason. Judas priest, these bastards rob banks and trains on a regular basis. Timing's everything. They wouldn't have let us catch them napping like this. So why are they trying to make us believe we did?'

'Been wondering the same thing.'

'And?'

'Best answer I can come up with is that this is a smokescreen.'

'Go on.'

'Sloane wants us to drop our guard for now.'

'Lull us to sleep by making us think we're safe?'

'Exactly. Then, once we're no longer vigilant, he'll take advantage of our vulnerability and pounce.'

'Makes sense,' Violet said. ' — if I just knew what vulnerability meant.'

She studied him shrewdly with her gold-flecked brown eyes. 'False humility doesn't suit you, Mr. Flowers. You're as educated as I am. And every bit as smart. For some reason you just don't like to admit it. Why is that, detective?'

''Mean why don't I use ten-dollar words?' Violet chuckled and for a moment listened to the wheels monotonously click-clacking on the rails. 'Well, way I see it, the more you can fit in, wherever you are, the more folks trust you. And the more folks trust you, the more information they're willing to share with you. And I learned a long time ago that a detective is only as good as his information.'

'Sounds logical.' Liberty gazed out the window at the passing scrubland. Flat as a lake, the drought-ridden ground was barren and devoid of its usual vast grasslands. In its place the rain-deprived soil was sparsely dotted with rocks and sun-bleached, shriveled plant life. The sight depressed her. 'God, I surely miss El Paso,' she said.

'There was always so much going on there — day or night.'

'I remember,' Violet said, his memories making him grin. 'Mostly the nights. I was only there for a short spell, but it's a time I won't easily forget.'

She looked at him curiously. 'Something tells me I don't want to hear what's making you smile.'

'Probably not.'

'Does Juarez have anything to do with it?'

'Ah, Juarez,' he sighed. 'Now you're talking. Been there, have you?'

'Once. With my father and Marshal Macahan, who was meeting up with his two brothers.'

'That sounds exciting.'

She ignored his sarcasm. 'When you've just turned seventeen, every new town's exciting — especially when it's in Mexico.'

'Reckon so . . . ' Violet dug out his tobacco pouch and fixings and started hand-rolling a smoke. 'Thing I remember most about Juarez is if a fella got bored in El Paso all he had to do was cross the river and he found himself in tequila heaven — '

'Or hell.'

' — where the senoritas were all beautiful and willing and the drinks never stopped coming.'

Liberty, aware of the blatant debauchery that went on in Juarez, felt a tinge of jealousy. The feeling was new and strange and it surprised her. She'd never cared enough about any man before to be jealous. And the fact that she did now when she had no real idea of how Violet felt about her, embarrassed her; made her feel vulnerable. She felt her cheeks flush, and hoping it wasn't noticeable she continued as if Juarez hadn't been mentioned.

'It's not just El Paso I miss, but Texas in general. I'm not from there — I was born and raised in New Mexico — but for some reason it always felt like home. Oh, I know in many ways the landscape's no different than here . . . and it's surely as hot. But seems like there was always plenty of good green grass and trees and plants that didn't look like God had cursed them.'

There was a trace of sadness in her voice that made Violet feel she missed more than just grass and trees. 'How about Drifter — your Pa, I mean — miss him, too, do you?'

'More than anything.' She sighed wistfully. 'He can be an awful headache at times, and stubborn beyond reason, but just having him around made me feel safe — needed — loved.'

Violet was briefly silent, then: 'Okay if I ask you a personal question?'

'Why aren't I married?'

'Reckon I'm more obvious than I thought.'

Liberty laughed good-naturedly. 'It's not you, Vi'. It's just . . . I get asked that all the time.'

'And what's your answer?'

Liberty shrugged. 'Getting married was never a high priority. I wanted this badge more than a wedding ring. Besides, time hasn't exactly passed me by. I'm still young. And I'm sure if the right man ever did come along . . . ' Her voice trailed off.'

'Sure that's all it is?'

'Isn't that reason enough?'

'Maybe. But my hunch is there's more to it than that.'

'Why? Can't a girl break the mold now and then without being considered a maverick?'

'Sure, in some cases.'

'But not mine?'

He shrugged his wide, rangy shoulders and studied her with narrowed, thoughtful eyes.

'If you've got a better reason,' Liberty said, 'I'd love to hear it.'

He thought a moment, gaze drifting to the window outside which the wasteland was no longer unrelentingly flat; now in places there were rocky outcrops and rugged ravines flanked by rolling sunburned hills.

'Well?' she said impatiently.

'Expectations.'

'You've lost me.'

'It's on account of your expectations.'

'Meaning?'

'You've set your sights on finding a fella who'll live up to your Pa and that's a mighty steep mountain to climb.'

She frowned, surprised and mildly irked by his suggestion.

'If you figure it's none of my business,' he said soberly, 'just tell me to button up.'

She didn't seem to hear him. Giving a long troubled sigh, she said: 'I never thought of it like that but I suppose you could be right.'

He remained silent, knowing she hadn't finished.

'I can tell you truthfully, though, that I don't remember ever consciously comparing anyone to my father.' She paused, bothered by her thoughts, then said: 'If you're right, and I'm not saying you are, is there something wrong with that?'

'Not wrong,' he said, 'but mighty limiting.'

'Oh?'

'Like I said before, other than Ezra Macahan I don't know anyone that compares favorably to your father. Men like him — men who place honor and integrity above all else — are rare, and getting rarer all the time.'

'Don't you think that's a bit unfair to the men of today or . . . tomorrow?'

'Could be . . . ' Violet paused to consider what he'd just said before saying: 'But the way I figure, it's not so much the men as the times. Civilization or progress, as the back-east bankers like to call it. They're equally to blame.'

'How so?'

'Thanks to the railroad, this land is opening up fast. Maybe too fast. Every day it's becoming more and more accessible to everyone. Towns and cities are springing up everywhere. And with each and every town and city come opportunities — more chances to be successful.'

'But surely that's a good thing?'

'Be nice to think so.'

'But you don't?'

He shrugged as if not sure. 'Trouble is, are men — and women too, I reckon — ready to discover El Dorado?' He took a long pull on his cigarette and then blew a smoke-ring that he burst with a stab of his finger. 'It'd take a fella much wiser than me to answer that. But from what little experience I've had in dealing with success and what it does to folks in general, it seems like for the most part success breeds more success, and more success breeds even more success and so on, until finally success turns into greed, uncontrollable greed that overpowers and buries most of the goodness in people.' He sighed heavily. 'I don't like to judge others and I dislike making broad sweeping statements, but from where I stand, seems like the more civilized a man gets, the more insatiable he — '

''Insatiable'?' she teased. 'Now who's using ten-dollar words?'

She expected him to be amused; instead he went on as if she hadn't spoken: 'I suppose it's only natural.

Folks see more, they want more. Hell, nowadays it's not enough for a fella to own a little spread, raise a family and maybe tend to some cattle or horses . . . he's got to have the biggest ranch or the biggest house around, and, by God, nothing's going to stop him from getting it — even if he has to step on his neighbors or break the law to get it.'

'Is that why you became a detective — to keep everyone honest?'

'Nope — though that's as good a reason as any. No, I became a detective — a railroad dick, as the Pinks like to say — for several reasons. 'Cause I'm good at it. 'Cause I can handle a gun and think around corners. And, lastly, 'cause I was born with vagabond shoes. Seldom a day goes by that I don't get an itch to travel. New places attract me like gold dust does a miner.'

'Then we're two of a kind,' Liberty said, pleased to have found a soul mate. 'I feel the same way about being a lawman. So long as there are people willing to break the law, I feel a need to arrest them — bring them to justice.'

Violet chuckled. 'Well, one thing's for sure — it ain't likely either of us will ever run out of work — ' He broke off as the train abruptly and violently put on the brakes. Steel screeched against steel. Cars lurched back and forth, threatening to jump the track, throwing passengers around in their seats, the whole train finally coming to a grinding, shuddering stop.

25

Shouts and panicked screams filled the passenger cars and everywhere frightened children could be heard crying.

Recovering quickly, Liberty and Violet grabbed their dropped rifles and trained them on the Wallace brothers. Though shaken, Josh was still in his seat but Caleb had been thrown to the floor. Blood ran down his face from a cut where his cheek had hit the corner of the seat opposite.

Violet one-handedly dragged him to his feet and pushed him back on the seat. 'Don't move,' he hissed, ' — either of you!'

Meanwhile, Clem came running up, rubbing the back of her head.

'You all right?' Liberty asked her.

Clem nodded. 'Just banged my head is all.' Looking through the window, where all she could see was scrubland

and rocky hills, she said fearfully: 'It's them, ain't it — my brothers?'

'I don't know,' Liberty said. 'Could be, but I haven't heard any shooting yet.' She moved to the window and pushed up the lower half. Poking her head out, she looked toward the engine. Ahead of her, many other passengers were also hanging out of their windows, all curious to see what was wrong.

Liberty leaned out even farther and at once saw the problem. A short distance beyond the hissing locomotive, a wide barricade of rocks lay across the tracks. Piled almost as high as a man, there were too many of them for the cow catcher to just ram through them.

Shading her eyes against the glaring sun, Liberty slowly searched the barricade for the outlaws she knew must be hiding behind it. But she couldn't see any sign of them.

The conductor now came running past, calling out, 'Stay inside, folks, stay inside,' heading for the locomotive. The engineer stood half-leaned out on the steps of the cab, waiting for the conductor to reach him.

Liberty looked at the barricade again and this time caught a glimpse of sunlight reflecting off a rifle barrel. An instant later it vanished as whoever was holding the weapon quickly lowered it behind the rocks.

Pulling her head back in, Liberty turned to Violet. Keeping her voice calm so as not to alarm anyone, she said: 'Stay here while I find out what's going on.' At the same time she gave him a warning look and nodded slightly so that he'd know she had seen danger ahead, danger that most likely was the Wallace gang. He nodded with his eyes to show he understood.

'Take care,' he said softly.

'Always.' She hurried off, elbowing her way through the passengers anxiously crowding the aisle, and disappeared out the forward door.

Josh gave a sneering laugh. 'Won't be long now,' he told Violet. 'Then we'll see who's getting their neck stretched.'

'I wouldn't count on that,' Violet warned. 'Like I told you before: I'd just as soon shoot you both than waste a good rope.'

26

As Liberty descended the steps of the narrow boarding platform, she noticed a blood spot and a tiny tuft of white fur on the metal floor. Wondering how they'd gotten there, she was about to hunker down to investigate — when shots rang out. They came from the direction of the barricade and she pulled back as bullets whined past her head. Waiting for the firing to stop, she peered cautiously around the side of the car in front of her.

Sunlight now reflected off several rifles resting atop the rocks and she caught glimpses of the outlaws firing them. There were only three of them and she didn't recognize their faces. Was this a coincidence, she wondered, a random train hold-up by bandits, or were they newcomers to the Wallace gang? And if so, where were the Wallace brothers themselves?

Before she could decide, she noticed a body sprawled facedown on the dirt alongside the locomotive. At first glance she'd thought it was a rock but as she took a closer look, she recognized the dark-blue uniform and realized it was the conductor. He wasn't moving and she cursed herself for being responsible for his death. She knew better than to let her conscience interfere with her job as a lawman; but she also knew that he was just doing his job too and that maybe if she hadn't been so damned stubborn, had tempered the law with common sense and released the Wallace brothers, as the sheriff and the mayor had wanted, the outlaws might have ridden on instead of hunting her down and the conductor would still be alive.

Another volley of shots interrupted her thinking.

Anger flared, replacing regret, and levering a shell into the chamber of her rifle she aimed around the side of the car and fired shot after shot at the outlaws. As she leaned back, out of the line of fire to reload, other shots came from behind her. Cautiously peering in the direction of the caboose, she saw Violet leaning out the window of the last passenger car, firing his rifle.

It was comforting to know he was there, that she could rely on him, and for the first time she found herself thinking that here at last was a man who could be favorably compared to her father; a man she might, *just might* respect enough — even learn to love enough to consider sharing the rest of her life with.

A bullet ricocheted off the car close to her head, startling her out of her reverie. Quickly levering in a round, she leaned forward so she could see the barricade and opened fire at the outlaws.

She'd emptied her magazine and was about to reload when she heard shots fired inside the car. She whirled around, intending to find out who'd fired them and saw, with heart-stopping dismay, a rifle pointed at her — a rifle held by a tall, dark-bearded, dark-browed, cruel-eyed man standing on the top step above her — a man she recognized from his wanted poster as the most dangerous outlaw in Oklahoma Territory.

'Know who I am?' he said softly.

Liberty nodded and forced herself not to show the fear she felt.

He smiled, a smile so full of cruelty her mouth went dry.

'Say it, girl. Say my name.'

'Sloane Wallace.'

He nodded, used one finger to push the flat-crowned black hat back off his forehead, and then made a fist with the same hand and punched her.

It was the first time she'd ever been punched in her life and she was totally unprepared for it. Her head snapped back, tiny lights flashed before her eyes and for a moment she felt an explosion of pain. Then everything went black and quiet and she fell sprawling backward onto the dirt.

27

When she regained consciousness, she had no idea where she was or why she was being jolted up and down. It took a few moments for her eyes to focus, and when they did she saw the ground was only a foot or two below her. Her mind spun a little, confused by her strange position, and then it dawned on her that she was hanging, face-down, over the back of a moving horse. Her jaw throbbed with pain and when she gingerly moved it around, it felt stiff and swollen. Ignoring the pain, she tried to shift positions, but couldn't. It was then she realized she was tied down by a cord that stretched from around her wrists, then under the belly of a horse to her ankles.

She could hear other horses trotting along beside her. Raising her head as far as her neck would allow she counted three riders. They were big, bearded, ill-clad gunmen whose faces, only half-seen below the brims of their sweat-stained Stetsons, belonged to members of the Wallace gang.

None of them were the Wallace brothers, and as she continued jolting along she wondered where they were — until she realized there were also riders on the other side of her horse; riders she couldn't see but, after listening carefully to the thudding hoof-beats, guessed numbered either five or six.

Since there were only five brothers, she wondered if the outlaws had also brought Clem or Violet along. Or, and this thought was painful to consider, if they both had resisted being taken prisoner and been killed. She didn't think it was likely that even Sloane would shoot his own sister, or step-sister, but anything was possible with this vicious, stone-hearted killer who on more than one occasion during robberies had gunned down whole families.

As for Violet Flowers, she didn't hold out much hope for his survival. He never would've surrendered quietly — and even if he had, she doubted if either Caleb or Josh Wallace would have let him live. They would've wanted payback for the way he'd treated them and that could only mean a bullet.

Saddened by the thought of losing a man she'd started to care for, Liberty tried to take her mind off his death by trying to figure out where they were.

Without being able to see the horizon it wasn't easy. But looking down, she saw that the soil passing quickly below her was dark-red and baked hard by a relentless summer sun and rutted in places by last winter's flash floods. She could be anywhere, she realized.

But as time and miles passed, she notice fan-shaped clumps of pale blue-green grass sprouting up. They had quill-like blades that ranged from several inches to more than a foot tall. She recalled that the locals called it

Little Bluestem grass, and she remembered having ridden this way before with Marshal Canada Thompson, when they had gone to arrest two half-breeds holed up in Canyon Country in the badlands. *So,* she thought, *we're back in Indian Territory!*

At the same time she reminded herself that the matriarch of the Wallace family, Ida-May 'Ma' Wallace, was supposedly living in a cabin somewhere in the Territory. Then it struck her. That was probably why the outlaws hadn't killed her: Ma Wallace wanted to inflict her own special punishment on the woman who had arrested her favorite son, Caleb.

The barking of a dog broke up her thoughts. It was a deep familiar bark and Liberty, though she couldn't see the dog, knew immediately it belonged to Trouble. But at the same time she knew that that was impossible. They had left the big white dog in the station-house at Clearwater, so how could it now be barking nearby?

A sudden shot, followed by a yelp, silenced the barking.

Liberty, realizing she would now never know the answer to her question, sighed and closed her eyes, trying as she did to forget the throbbing pain that with each jolting step of the horse wracked her swollen jaw.

28

Having lost all sense of time during the long painful ride, Liberty had no idea how far they'd traveled or in which direction once they'd crossed into Indian Territory — until it occurred to her that their shadows might tell her.

Sweat dripping from her face, she forced herself to forget how thirsty she was and gazed numbly at the dirt. She saw that the shadows made by herself and the horse were on her side and almost directly beneath her. That meant the sun was still climbing in the east but close to being overhead, making it around noon. It also meant they were heading west or southwest, basically in the same direction that she and Marshal Thompson had ridden when they had gone after Willie Gray Eyes and Sam Growling Bear, two half-breeds who'd jumped the reservation

231

and killed a bartender in Clearwater for refusing to serve them whiskey.

The renegades had holed up in one of the numerous caves in Canyon Country, and when she and the marshal had finally tracked them down by following the tracks made by a cracked shoe on one of their ponies, they'd refused to surrender and Marshal Thompson had been forced to kill them in the ensuing shootout.

Now, as her horse and the others around her slowed to a walk and finally reined up, she heard three pistol shots, one right after the other like a signal, followed by Sloane's voice as he called out:

'Ma . . . Ma, it's me an' the boys! You hear me?'

'I hear you,' a woman's voice replied.

'Don't shoot! We're coming in . . .'

'Come ahead,' the woman said. 'But make it nice'n slow, so's I can see your every move.' The voice was harsh, raspy and belligerently domineering. But Liberty also detected a sense of edgy suspicion and wondered if Ma Wallace, tough as she was, was so paranoid she didn't trust her own sons.

A moment later Liberty felt her horse being pulled forward by the rider in front of her. She tried not to be afraid, reassuring herself that though Federal Marshals did get shot on occasion, it was usually under desperate kill-or-be-killed circumstances. Otherwise, unlike local sheriffs, who got shot far more frequently, outlaws hesitated to gun down a Federal officer as they knew they would be relentlessly hunted down by government-sponsored posses and killed on the spot or hung after a speedy and not necessarily judicious trial.

But this was Indian Territory, lawless and dangerous, and Ma Wallace was a vicious, vindictive woman who dealt out her own justice, and Liberty knew her chances of survival weren't good. She tried to swallow her fear but her throat was too parched and what little saliva she mustered remained in her mouth, sour and coppery-tasting.

★ ★ ★

The old two-room log cabin was solid as a fort. It sat across from a small barn and corral in a cup-shaped hollow in a narrow, steep-walled canyon, protected on three sides by sheer cliffs that also helped shield it from the blazing sun. A few leafless, half-dead trees failed to conceal the front of the cabin. But that didn't matter. It could only be approached by a narrow descending trail that was clearly visible from both the door and tiny window of the cabin. As such it was easy to defend; anyone capable of shooting a repeating rifle could hold off an army for as long as their food and ammunition lasted — and Ma Wallace made sure she always had plenty of both.

Now, as everyone dismounted and Liberty was untied and roughly pulled from her horse, she got her first glimpse of the Wallace family matriarch.

It was not a comforting sight. Ma was

234

a large, raw-boned woman with a pock-marked face ugly as a pan of worms. She had straggly brown hair, beetle brows and cruel blue eyes. Her skin was leathery and the same color brown as her sackcloth dress. A clay pipe poked out of her pocket and the left side of her face was stained yellow by nicotine. But it was her mouth that most people remembered. Small and pinched, she had thin mean lips that rarely smiled and no one could ever remember hearing her laugh.

She approached Liberty, standing close enough for Liberty to smell her sour onion-breath, and sized her up as if she were meat for the pot.

'You're her, ain't you?' she rasped. 'The one who think she's the law?'

Her tone was insulting and belittling, and anger replaced Liberty's fear.

'I don't *think* I'm the law, Mrs. Wallace. I *am* the law.'

'Well, now, we'll see 'bout that, won't we?' Ma turned to Sloane, who stood holding Clem by her arm. 'Where's

Colton and the Harvick twins?'

'All feet up.'

'How?'

'They was hid behind these rocks we piled up to stop the train, and got killed by this tall fella who was in the same car as her,' he thumbed at Clem.

Ma scowled in disgust. 'You let one man kill three of ours?'

Sloane shrugged. 'Happened afore we boarded the train.'

'He won't be killing nobody else, Ma,' Caleb grinned. 'I shot him when Virge cut me'n Josh loose.'

'Good boy.'

'Still wish we'd stayed to make sure he was dead,' Josh grumbled.

'Dead — dying — what's the difference?' Caleb said.

'Plenty. One's permanent, the other's maybe.'

'Maybe? Hell, you saw the bastard drop, same as me. What's 'maybe' about that?'

'Quit jawing, you two,' Ma snapped. Then to Sloane: 'Who was he?'

''Cording to Caleb, he worked for the railroad.'

'If you don't believe me, Ma, ask her,' Caleb said, pointing at Liberty. 'She was sweet on him.'

'That true, marshal? Was this fella your beau?'

'Absolutely not. We just met.'

'That's the truth, Ma,' Clem said. 'Liberty and me was in Spader's Livery and this drunk who was sleeping it off up in the hay, he heard us talking.'

Ma Wallace gave Clem a cruel withering look, 'Shut your yap, child. You already in enough trouble,' and then glared at Liberty. 'If this man was a drunk, why'd you take him along?'

'He wasn't a drunk,' Liberty said. 'He was a railroad detective working under-cover. And I didn't 'take him along,' he insisted on accompanying me.'

'Yeah, so's he could help you arrest us,' Caleb blurted. ''Cause he knew you couldn't have corralled us on your own — you being a woman an' all.'

Liberty turned to Ma. 'Cut me loose

and give us both a gun,' she seethed, 'and let's see who ends up being corralled.'

Ma eyed her curiously. 'Got grit, girl, I'll give you that. But I got other plans for you.' She stuck her pipe in her mouth but didn't light it. 'Take her inside,' she told Sloane, 'and make damn' sure she's tied up good.'

'What about her?' he said, thumbing at Clem.

'Tie her up, too.'

'Ain't you gonna whip her good?' Caleb said, disappointed.

'All in good time, son.' Ma took a closer look at Liberty, adding: 'How'd your jaw get all swolled like that?'

'Ask him,' Liberty said, eyeing Sloane. 'Seems that bullying women runs in your family.'

'She asked for it,' Sloane said. 'Kept runnin' that smart mouth of hers. Now, get on inside,' he pushed Liberty in the back, hard enough to make her stumble, and she grudgingly entered the cabin. Sloane and Clem followed.

29

Inside, the cabin was sparingly furnished and surprisingly neat and clean. Very little light came in through the small, shuttered window and the whole place smelled of stale pipe tobacco and pan-fried cooking.

Sloane forced Liberty and Clem to sit in the corner facing the old iron stove, and then bound their hands and feet with rawhide. He was rough with them and tied the rawhide so tight it cut into their skin. When he was finished, he smiled mockingly at them, expecting them to whine or plead with him to loosen their bonds. But Liberty, determined not to let him know his sadistic behavior was affecting her, kept silent and with her eyes signaled to Clem to do the same.

Clem went one better, poking her tongue out at him as he started to leave.

Infuriated, he kicked her twice in the ribs, making her yelp, and then stormed out.

'Shouldn't have done that,' Liberty chided, though inwardly admiring the child's defiance. 'You'll only rile him up and then he'll take a whip to you.'

'Ma's gonna do that anyway,' Clem said. 'Like Pa always used to say: May as well be hung for a sheep as a lamb.'

Liberty chuckled, despite herself, and tried to reach the knot binding the rawhide about her wrists. It was impossible. Shifting onto her side, she turned her back toward Clem, saying: 'See if you can untie me.'

Clem inched herself backward, until she was almost against Liberty. She then groped around, trying to feel for the knot with her outstretched fingers. It took a few minutes to find it, then several more minutes as she struggled to loosen the knotted rawhide. It, too, was impossible.

'Sorry,' she said, finally giving up. 'I tried. I really did. But it's just too tight.'

There was frustration and fear in her voice. Liberty sat up and kissed her on the cheek. 'Don't worry,' she said gently. 'We'll find a way to get out of this. You'll see . . . '

Clem didn't answer for a few moments. Then sniffing back tears, she said: 'S'all my fault.'

'Don't be silly,' Liberty said, misunderstanding. 'If anyone's to blame, it's me. I shouldn't have brought you along in the first place. Should've taken the time to find someone in town to look after you.'

'That ain't what I mean,' Clem said. 'I'm talking about Mr. Flowers.'

'What about him?'

'He saw my other brothers getting on the train. Could've shot 'em easy as they come through the rear door — '

'Why didn't he?'

''Cause of me. Seeing Sloane threw a scare into me and I tried to run. But my feet got all tangled up and I fell. I got up straightaway but as I did, my back was to Josh and he jumped me, knocking me to the floor. Mr. Flowers, he tried to pull him off and . . . and that's when Caleb somehow got his hands free and grabbed his gun, Mr. Flowers' gun I mean, and — '

'Shot him?'

Clem nodded and tears welled in her eyes.

'It's all right,' Liberty soothed. 'No one's blaming you. That's what Mr. Flowers was supposed to do — protect you — you and all the other passengers on the train. It's what he gets — got paid for . . . ' She broke off as the thought of Violet being dead caught up with her, choking off the words in her throat.

But dismayed as she was, her survival instincts refused to let her dwell on his death. Fighting down her emotions, she immediately tried to think of ways to escape. She gazed about her, looking for something that might provide a means of getting loose before Ma Wallace or one of her sons entered the cabin.

What she saw wasn't promising: crudely made furniture, wood-burning stove next to the pantry, cheap crucifix hanging by the window, a Winchester Model '73 carbine resting on a deer rack over the front door and — wait! — something clicked in her mind and her gaze returned to the deer rack. The gun was too high for her to reach, unless her hands were free and she stood on a chair, but the wide-spread antlers gave her an idea.

'While you were growing up,' she said to Clem, 'did you and your family eat a lot of fresh venison?'

'Venison?'

'Deer meat.'

'Oh-h . . . Yeah . . . Mostly that's all we ate. That'n beans and flour biscuits and sometimes ham or bacon when we had hogs. Pa loved bacon. Oh, and eggs, he loved eggs too, and so did I. But the hawks and coyotes kept killing off the chickens, so — '

'Never mind the chickens,' Liberty interrupted. 'Where's your Ma keep her

243

sharp knives — you know, for cutting meat?'

'In that drawer over there,' Clem nodded at three drawers built below a counter in the kitchen area. ' — the top one.'

Liberty quickly tucked her legs under her, struggled to her knees and then with great effort, managed to stand up. Ankles tightly bound, she hopped to the drawers and turned around so her hands could reach the top drawer. It took a few moments but after several fumbling attempts, she pulled it open. Keeping her back to the drawer, she groped around inside until she grasped the buck-horn handle of a carving knife. She then held the blade upward and sawed the sharp edge against the rawhide binding her wrists.

Soon she was free. Rubbing the circulation back into her hands, she bent down, cut her ankles loose and then hurried over beside Clem. 'Quick. Hurry. Turn around!'

Clem obeyed and Liberty cut her

free. 'Where's your Ma keep the ammo for that carbine?'

'Bedroom closet . . . on a shelf.'

'Bring me what you can find while I get the gun down.'

'Sure.' Clem ran into the bedroom. Liberty dragged a chair over to the door, climbed onto it and grabbed the carbine off the rack. Jumping down, she went to the window and peered out through the rifle-slot in the shutters.

Outside, Ma, her five sons and the other outlaws stood talking by the barn. All the men had bedrolls under their arm and Liberty guessed that other than Ma, and maybe Clem, everyone else bedded down in the barn.

'This is all there was,' Clem said, holding up an almost full box of 44–40 caliber cartridges.

'That's fine.' Liberty dragged the table over by the window and dumped the cartridges out on it. 'Any other guns around, do you know?'

'Uh-uh.'

'No matter — '

'I still got my old bow an' arrows — '

'Bow and arrows?'

'Yeah. They're in Ma's closet. I just saw 'em.'

'Can you hit anything with them?'

'Sure. Used to kill jackrabbits all the time.'

'Go get them.' As Clem hurried into the bedroom, Liberty wedged one of the chairs against the door then returned to the window and peered through the slot. Satisfied that nothing had changed outside, she made sure the carbine was fully loaded and then leaned it against the wall, ready to use the moment Ma or anyone approached the cabin.

Clem rejoined her shortly carrying an Osage orangewood bow, already strung, and a doeskin quiver filled with arrows. Liberty pulled out one of the arrows and inspected its hand-chipped, razor-sharp flint head. 'You made this?' she said, impressed.

'Uh-huh. And the bow. This old Cherokee Pa knew — Sam Long Nose

— showed me how. Taught me how to shoot, too. An' how to trap eagles so I could kill 'em for their feathers.'

Liberty gently ran her finger along the edge of one of the three feathers neatly bound to the nock-end of the arrow, admiring the workmanship.

'You're a remarkable young lady,' she said quietly — then quickly turned to the window as voices approached the cabin. 'It's your Ma and Caleb,' she whispered to Clem.

'What're we gonna do?'

In answer Liberty grabbed the carbine, levered a round into the chamber and poked the barrel out through the slot in the shutters.

'Kill Ma first,' Clem said bitterly. 'Without her giving orders, my brothers will be like a snake with its head cut off.'

Ignoring her Liberty squeezed off a round, the bullet kicking up dirt in front of Ma's feet. She and Caleb jumped back, startled, and for a moment stood there, frozen.

'Next bullet's for Caleb, Mrs. Wallace,' Liberty called out. 'And I can promise you, at this range I won't miss.'

Ma glowered but knew she was a dead cigar. 'What do you want?' she demanded.

'A ticket out of here.'

'Go on.'

'For Clem *and* me. Oh, and two horses.'

'Don't trust her,' hissed Clem. 'She'd sooner lie than spit.'

'Why should I let you go?' Ma said. 'Even if you do kill Caleb, and me too, my other boys will burn you out of there and see that you die real slow.'

'Maybe,' said Liberty. 'But more than one of them will die before that happens. Soon as they show their heads out of that barn, I'll pick them off like sitting ducks. You want that?' she added before Ma could reply. ' — for your sons to die just so you can have the pleasure of killing me?'

Ma shifted uneasily on her feet. Beside her, Caleb nervously licked his snuff-stained lips and glanced at the barn, wondering if it was close enough to risk running.

'Do like she says, Ma,' he urged. 'We can always kill her some other time. Clem, too.'

'Shut up, boy! Let me think.' Pausing, Ma finally said to Liberty: 'If I let you go, and I ain't saying I will, you gotta leave Clem behind.'

'No deal. Clem goes with me. That's final.'

Behind Ma, the barn door opened a crack and Sloane peered out. Liberty fired at him. The bullet chipped wood from the door inches above his head, driving him back inside.

'Well, what's it going to be?' she shouted. 'You want to bury me or three or four of your sons?'

Rage whitened Ma's lined, weathered face.

'You win,' she said grudgingly. 'Come on out.'

Liberty almost laughed. 'You must take me for a fool, Mrs. Wallace. The only way I'm coming out is when everyone in that barn is lined up alongside you — without their guns. Then I want someone to saddle up two horses and bring them out and leave them in front of the cabin, so Clem and I have a clear path to ride out of here. Anything short of that, I don't come out and you can have the joy of burying your youngest son and whoever else dies.'

For the longest time Ma stood there, motionless except for the rage seething through her. Finally she sagged, as if broken, and looked over her shoulder at the barn.

'Do as she says, boys. Drop your irons and come on out. And bring two horses with you. Don't forget to saddle 'em, neither.' Turning back to the cabin, she added: 'Satisfied, marshal?'

'It's a start,' Liberty said. 'But I won't be satisfied till you and your evil brood is locked behind bars.'

30

The burning hatred on Ma's face as she watched Liberty cautiously walk out of the cabin, rifle in hand with Clem a step behind her, would have frightened the devil.

Sullenly lined up beside her, her sons and the other outlaws looked almost as menacing.

Liberty could almost feel their rage and frustration as she led Clem to the two saddled horses standing nearby. Never once did she take her eyes off Ma Wallace or her sons, or her finger off the trigger of her rifle. She felt sweat trickling down her back under her shirt. It was hot and there were no clouds to hide the blazing sun. But she knew the sweat wasn't caused by the heat; in the dead of winter with snow on the ground, she would have still been sweating.

But she also knew fear wasn't always a bad thing. As Marshals Macahan and Thompson had drummed into her — as long as she kept her nerves under control, her actions calm and her thinking straight, fear could work in her favor. Almost everyone felt fearful in desperate situations. The trick was to control it. Controlled fear heightened one's senses, forcing them to stay alert, to be ever-cautious and aware of the danger confronting them.

She felt that way now as they reached the horses. 'You first,' she told Clem. 'And remember, don't — '

' — get between you and Ma or my brothers,' Clem finished, 'yeah, I remember.' Slinging her bow and quiver over her back, Indian-style, she grasped the reins and swung up into the saddle.

'Better hope me or your brothers don't ever set eyes on you again,' Ma warned her. ''Cause if we do, child, you'll surely regret bein' born.'

'Wouldn't be nothin' new,' Clem said

flatly. 'I wished I hadn't been born all the time I was living here after you killed Pa.'

'Quiet,' Liberty said. 'Never mind them. Concentrate on what you're supposed to be doing.'

Clem fell silent and sat there, astride the gray gelding, glaring sullenly at Ma and her brothers.

A wind sprang up, moaning through the canyon and blowing dust and dead brush around everyone's ankles.

Liberty's horse whinnied and shied nervously. She jerked on the reins, pulling the skittish horse close so that it didn't block her view of Ma or the outlaws and then stepped up into the saddle. She moved deliberately, in graceful slow-motion, never once taking her eyes from her enemies.

Once mounted, she was certain she had everything under control. But as she nudged the horse forward, her gaze still fixed on Ma and the outlaws, she glimpsed something moving to her right. Instinctively she glanced that way, at the same time raising the Winchester to shoot, realizing too late that it was merely the wind blowing the barn door open.

For an instant her attention was diverted from the outlaws and in that instant several things happened almost at once, each one seemingly triggering the next:

Ma reached for the belly gun tucked inside the folds of her dress —

Liberty swung the rifle around to shoot her —

Sloane Wallace hurled himself at Liberty's horse, grasped her leg and tried to pull her from the saddle —

The startled horse reared up, almost unseating Liberty and knocking her rifle upward, causing her to fire into the air —

Lee Wallace grasped the reins of Clem's horse. The frightened gelding suddenly side-stepped, throwing Clem to the ground —

Caleb dived on top of her and started to strangle her —

Lastly, something large and white sprang, snarling, from behind a nearby rock. Moving with blurring speed, it knocked Caleb off Clem and sent him sprawling.

Liberty was the first to recover. Controlling her horse, she clubbed Sloane with the butt of her Winchester, smashing him to the ground.

Meanwhile, Trouble had straddled Caleb, biting his arms as he frantically tried to protect his throat, his screams echoing through the canyon.

Ma, to her credit, ran to him, cursing the dog while trying to drag it off her favorite son.

But she was too late. Trouble's jaws had crushed Caleb's windpipe and the Great Pyrenees now turned to attack Ma.

She staggered back, managing as she did to pull out her belly gun. She fired twice. But in her haste, both bullets only grazed the dog, angering it even further. Snarling, it charged her. Ma fired again. This time the bullet grazed

Trouble's shoulder, causing the dog to stumble.

Ma went to shoot it, but before she could an arrow buried in her shoulder. With a cry of pain she dropped the gun, whirled around and saw Clem, bow in hand, fumbling for another arrow.

Enraged, Ma came lumbering toward her.

Panicking, Clem dropped the bow and ran.

By now the rest of the outlaws had scattered, most of them running into the barn to collect their weapons.

Liberty calmly shot two of them. Then seeing Clem struggling in the grip of her step-brother Virge, she spurred her horse at him. The animal struck Virge with its shoulder, slamming him to the dirt. Liberty shot him, spun her horse around and stretched out her hand, 'Here!' pulling Clem up behind her.

As she did several outlaws burst out of the barn, all firing at her.

Liberty felt her horse stagger and

knew it had been hit. She took quick aim at the outlaws, pumping shot after shot at them. Two of them went down and a third stumbled back, wounded, but continued firing at her.

Liberty saw it was Lee Wallace. She shot him again, killing him, and then felt her horse buckle beneath her. 'Jump!' she yelled.

Clem obeyed, leaping clear. But before Liberty could get her boot out of the stirrup, the horse went down and she went with it.

Liberty felt intense pain shooting up the leg buried under the fallen horse and guessed it was broken. She tried to pull herself free from the dying animal, but was pinned by its weight. She desperately kept trying, unaware for the moment that all the shooting had ceased. Then the horse stopped flailing around and she heard its last wheezing breath.

Suddenly the canyon was strangely silent except for the faint moaning of the wind.

Clem appeared beside her — hair in disarray and her dirt-smudged face filled with fear as she struggled to break loose from Ma's grip.

31

'Well, now,' Ma said, looking down at Liberty. 'Seems to me, deputy, your string's played out.' Turning to Sloane, who was bleeding from the blow Liberty had delivered to his head, she added: 'Get her out from under there, son. We got business with her.'

'Sure, Ma.' Sloane signaled for the remaining outlaws to help him, and together they pulled the dead horse aside and dragged Liberty to her feet.

Pain again shot up Liberty's left leg, but she was able to put her weight on it without it buckling and felt relieved to know it wasn't broken.

Ma leaned her sweaty face in close. 'Three of my boys is dead,' she said grimly. ''Fore today's over, deputy, you're gonna beg me to let you join 'em. As for you,' she added, turning to Clem, 'your pain's 'bout to begin.'

'I ain't afraid of you,' Clem said defiantly. 'Even if you was to kill me it don't matter. 'Cause then I'll be with Pa again — '

Ma backhanded her, rocking Clem's head back. She went to slap her again — then abruptly stopped in mid-swing as a shot rang out. She staggered back, a shocked look on her weathered, pock-marked face as she looked down and saw the reddening hole in her chest.

Liberty and everyone around her whirled and looked up the canyon — where three riders approached along the narrow descending trail. All were armed with rifles, ready to shoot the first outlaw that moved.

Recognizing them, Liberty grew almost giddy with relief.

Sloane, also recognizing the riders, knew his life was over and jerked his six-gun. It barely cleared leather before another shot echoed through the canyon and Sloane went down in a sprawling heap.

The rider who'd fired, a tall, heavy-shouldered, gray-haired man in a dark suit and black string tie, levered another round into the chamber and raised the Winchester to his shoulder.

'Rope or bullet,' Marshal Ezra Macahan said bluntly, 'makes no matter to me how you go out.'

'Me, either,' said the rider alongside him. He was about the same age and height as the lawman but leaner, and his long dark hair was tinted with silver.

'Fact is, be a whole sight less trouble if all you bastards were dead.'

The third rider, who was younger, more affable looking and had his right arm in a sling, said nothing. But the look on his tanned, stubbly face clearly showed that his sentiments were the same.

Josh Wallace and the few remaining outlaws needed only a moment to decide. Then, as one, they dropped their guns, raised their hands and watched as the three riders rode slowly toward them.

'Look! It's him!' exclaimed Clem, pointing at the rider whose arm was in a sling. 'Mr. Flowers!'

'I know,' Liberty said, equally pleased. 'Guess your brother Caleb was wrong after all.'

'Who's that other fella?' Clem said, looking at the man riding beside Marshal Macahan. 'Way he's looking at you, it seems like he knows you.'

'Indeed he does,' Liberty said wryly. She smiled at the man whom everyone called Drifter. 'He's my father.'

32

'There ain't much more to tell,' Violet said. He stopped looking out the cabin window and sat at the kitchen table across from Liberty. 'Soon as the tracks were cleared and the train got to Guthrie, I had Doc Masters patch up my arm and then I told Marshal Thompson and Ezra what had happened — '

'Wait,' Liberty said. 'What was Marshal Macahan doing in Guthrie?'

'He'd ridden up from El Paso with a prisoner. Like you and me, he was hoping Judge Parker would find him guilty and string him up.'

'What about Marshal Thompson — why didn't he come with you?'

'He wanted to. But he had business with the governor and Ezra offered to take his place.'

'And my father?'

'What about him?'

'Why was he in town?'

'Beats me.'

'Quit lying,' Liberty said impatiently. 'You're no good at it.'

'I'm not — '

'I mean it, Vi'. I want to know what my dad was doing in Guthrie.'

Violet shrugged. 'Keeping Ezra company, I reckon.'

'You can do better than that.'

'Look, instead of badgering me, why don't you go ask him yourself? He's outside.'

'Maybe I will.' Liberty got to her feet, went to the door, opened it and looked out.

A few feet away Clem was sitting on the ground, one arm happily draped around Trouble. The great white dog's shoulder fur was caked with dry blood. Otherwise, it seemed fine.

Beyond Clem, not far from the barn, Drifter stood, smoking, Winchester resting on his shoulder, while he and Marshal Macahan watched the outlaws digging graves for the dead.

'He was there to chase the rabbit, wasn't he?' Liberty said, turning back to Violet. 'Figured since I was busy in Clearwater, I wouldn't find out.'

'You make it sound like he don't have the right.'

'Do I? I don't mean to. It's just I love him dearly and he's not a kid anymore — '

'I'd hate to be the one telling him that,' Violet said. 'He might get a tad salty and that'd be a whole lot more trouble than I could handle.'

'You men,' Liberty grumbled. 'Why can't you act your age?'

'Mean grow old gracefully?'

'Exactly.'

'Like when women gussy up their hair and put on more rouge and powder to hide their lines?'

Liberty had to smile. 'Fair enough . . . ' Closing the door, she came and stood in front of him, adding: 'Speaking of getting on in years, I'll be twenty-something soon and — '

'You're already twenty-something.'

She chuckled. 'Reckon I deserved that.'

'Amen.'

'Well, you don't have to be so damned smug about it.'

Violet grinned and studied her as if trying to figure something out.

'What?' she said, hand straying to her nose. 'Do I have dirt on my — ?'

'No, no, I was just thinking 'bout something else your father said.'

'About me?'

Violet hesitated, unwilling to say.

'Well?' she demanded. 'Was it?'

Realizing he'd trapped himself, he said: 'I'm sure he didn't mean it.'

Liberty bristled. 'My father's never said anything he didn't mean for as long as I've known him. It isn't his nature. Like Marshal Macahan says: 'Your Daddy don't know the meaning of tact.' And he's right. So unless you want me to think you're covering for him — '

'Okay, okay,' Violet said. 'If you must

know your name happened to come up while we were following your tracks from where the train was attacked. We'd stopped for water and Drifter asked me how I'd met you. When I told him 'bout how you wanted to steal my horse — '

'Commandeer it — '

' — and wouldn't take no for an answer, he grinned and said he wasn't surprised. Said you were bossy even as a young'un.'

'Sounds like my dad.'

'Also said you were more bullheaded than — '

'Even he was?'

'Something like that.'

'It's more like a tie,' Liberty said. 'But even if he's right, when you're a woman trying to enforce the law in Indian Territory it pays to be a little bullheaded.'

'Can't argue with that.'

They were both silent a moment. Outside, the noise of shovels biting in the sun-baked dirt was almost rhythmic.

'Look,' Liberty said suddenly, 'what I started to say was, I know it's not exactly ladylike to throw yourself at a man, but will I be seeing you again?'

Violet got up and put his good arm around her waist. 'Unless you tell me different.'

Liberty smiled. 'No fear of that.'

'Good.'

'But I wouldn't want us to rush things, either.'

'Rush things?'

'Yes, you know. We both have our careers and we both work in different territories, which means we probably won't see each other very often, so — '

'Stop right there,' Violet said, adding: 'I'm not Latigo Rawlins.'

Her mouth dropped. 'W-What?'

'You don't have to worry about making the same mistake twice.'

'Meaning?'

'I ain't asking you to sneak out of a convent to see me on the sly or . . . elope to Mexico.'

Now she was really shocked. 'H-How

do you know about that? Oh my God,' she said before he could reply. 'Of course! My father.'

'We may have shared a few words about your past,' Violet admitted.

'*A few words?* Hell's bells, sounds like he told you my whole life story!'

'Wouldn't go as far as to say that.'

'Damn him, he had no right.'

'No right?' Violet smiled wryly, 'Let me see now . . . ' and began ticking off his fingers. 'He can't chase the rabbit — can't sell the ranch — can't talk about his daughter — whom he adores and thinks is wonderful, by the way — seems to me, deputy, being your father's 'bout as much fun as kissing a rattlesnake. I mean is there anything he *can* do that doesn't piss you off?'

Stung, Liberty reddened. 'That's not fair! My father can do anything he damn' well wants — and does, believe me. In fact most of what I say goes in one ear and out the other. So don't bury him yet, Mr. Flowers.'

'I ain't trying to — '

'What's more, I think you're being very presumptuous and I don't appreciate it. Don't appreciate it one bit. Just because we like each other, find each other attractive, doesn't give you the right to pass judgment on me or the way I treat my — '

Violet pressed his finger over her lips, silencing her. 'Want to know what else your father said about you?'

'I dread to think.'

'You talk too much.'

'Then stop me,' she said, tilting her face up to his.

He did. He kissed her.

THE END

We do hope that you have enjoyed reading this large print book.

Did you know that all of our titles are available for purchase?

We publish a wide range of high quality large print books including:
Romances, Mysteries, Classics
General Fiction
Non Fiction and Westerns

Special interest titles available in large print are:
The Little Oxford Dictionary
Music Book, Song Book
Hymn Book, Service Book

Also available from us courtesy of Oxford University Press:
Young Readers' Dictionary
(large print edition)
Young Readers' Thesaurus
(large print edition)

For further information or a free brochure, please contact us at:
Ulverscroft Large Print Books Ltd.,
The Green, Bradgate Road, Anstey,
Leicester, LE7 7FU, England.
Tel: (00 44) 0116 236 4325
Fax: (00 44) 0116 234 0205

GONE TO BLAZES

Jackson Davis

In the Longhorn saloon in the rambunctious gold rush town of White Oaks, New Mexico, young sawyer Vince falls for the beautiful dancer Selina. But he stands no chance against Texan killer Cotton Bulloch, who kidnaps and brutally forces himself on her. Meanwhile, Jake Blackman and his boys flood the area with forged greenbacks. Can Sheriff Pat Garrett put paid to both Bulloch and Blackman? Must Vince face the murderous Texan alone? And is his love for Selina doomed?